THE HAUNTING OF ALICE FAIRLIE

EILEEN DUNLOP

POOLBEG
FOR CHILDREN

Published 2001
by Poolbeg Press Ltd
123 Baldoyle Industrial Estate
Dublin 13, Ireland
E-mail: poolbeg@poolbeg.com
www.poolbeg.com

© Eileen Dunlop 2001

Copyright for typesetting, layout, design
© Poolbeg Group Services Ltd.

1 3 5 7 9 10 8 6 4 2

The moral right of the author has been asserted.

A catalogue record for this book is available from the British Library.

ISBN 1 85371 973 0

All rights reserved. No part of this publication may be reproduced or
transmitted in any form or by any means, electronic or mechanical,
including photography, recording, or any information storage or retrieval
system, without permission in writing from the publisher. The book is sold
subject to the condition that it shall not, by way of trade or otherwise, be
lent, resold or otherwise circulated without the publisher's prior consent in
any form of binding or cover other than that in which it is published and
without a similar condition, including this condition, being imposed on the
subsequent purchaser.

Cover design by Slatter-Anderson
Typeset by Patricia Hope in Goudy 12/15
Printed by The Guernsey Press Ltd,
Vale, Guernsey, Channel Islands

20056148
MORAY COUNCIL
LIBRARIES &
INFORMATION SERVICES
JC

Acknowledgement

The author is glad to acknowledge the help of Andrew Hunt, Principal Teacher of History at Alloa Academy, who gave her generous access to the archive of her old school.

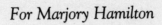

For Marjory Hamilton

Contents

1

I, Alice Fairlie

When Grandma came to lunch on the last Christmas Day we'd ever spend together as a family, she gave me a book called *Lorna Doone*. It was by somebody called R.D. Blackmore, and the minute I saw the picture on the cover – a woman in a long frilly dress and a guy in breeches and a silly hat with a feather – I knew that my hints about wanting the new Terry Pratchett had been ignored.

"It was a favourite of mine when I was your age," said Grandma, making my heart sink. I'd heard the same last year when she gave me *A Tale of Two Cities* and the year before when she gave me *Ivanhoe*.

Of course, I didn't blame Grandma. When she was young, there was nothing to do but read. People actually enjoyed books six hundred pages long, in tiny type and with sentences that lasted half a page. And I wouldn't have hurt Grandma's feelings, especially on Christmas Day. After lunch, when Mum, Dad and Grandma were watching television and my big sister Shirley was gassing on the phone upstairs, I sat in a corner pretending that I couldn't put the book down.

Actually, I hated *Lorna Doone*. Reading it was like trying to swim through porridge. I got bogged down in the long sentences and I didn't care what happened to people who lived three hundred years ago. When Dad took Grandma home in the evening, I chucked the book in my bedroom cupboard. I don't even know what happened to it in the terrible upheaval that followed. But I've always remembered how the first chapter began – probably because it wasn't true.

"If anybody cares to read a simple tale told simply, I, John Ridd, have seen and had a share in some doings of this neighbourhood, which I will try to set down in order . . ."

If *Lorna Doone* was simple, I was missing something. But now that I'm the one with a tale to tell, and the need inside me to write it down, I know that the hardest thing is deciding how to start. So thanks, John Ridd.

If anybody cares to read a weird tale told simply, I, Alice Fairlie, have seen and had a share in some doings of another neighbourhood . . . beginning one wild and wet November. I was thirteen years old and both my parents were dead. I was so unhappy, I thought I wanted to be dead too.

2

What the Cat Saw

I never was the sort of person who was scared of ghosts. At primary school, if the teacher asked at Hallowe'en, "Who believes in ghosts?", I was the one who grinned sceptically when other kids put up their hands. Moving from Glasgow to Millkennet changed all that. From the moment I walked through the door of 2 Goldie Court, I knew there was something not right about the place. It didn't matter how often I told myself that even if ghosts did exist they were unlikely to haunt a new apartment block, I kept hearing whispers and giggles. Doors banged when there was no draught. Things definitely went bump in the night.

My cat Sooty wasn't happy either. At home in Glasgow he'd been a placid, lazy animal. Since we'd moved to Millkennet he'd been acting like a witch's cat, with arched back, stiff tail and eyes glaring like green lamps. I was convinced he was seeing things I couldn't see. Of course I didn't mention any of this to Shirley. Feeling haunted is hard to explain and no one likes to sound ridiculous.

The last Friday in November began as another sad,

lonely day. I should have been at school, but I'd had a terrible night. Every time I dozed off I had a bad dream, from which I was startled by the thunder of a train passing nearby. By the time my alarm beeped at half-past seven, my tummy ached and I couldn't keep my eyes open. The idea of sitting through French, Physics and Maths was even less appealing than the prospect of being alone in the apartment all day. I crawled miserably out of bed, dragged on my dressing-gown and sloped into the kitchen.

"Shirley, I feel awful," I whined, slumping onto a chair. "Don't make me go to school."

Shirley gave me a dark look. As she whirled round the kitchen, drinking coffee, making toast, putting on her eye make-up at a mirror on top of the fridge, I could see her arguing with herself. Should she be hard-hearted and boot me out, or should she give in, yet again? Since I'd started at Millkennet High School in mid-August, I'd been absent for at least one day in most weeks. This embarrassed Shirley, who taught English at the school and probably had to endure snide comments from my class tutor, Granny Clark. She didn't like leaving me alone either, but she didn't know any of our neighbours well enough to ask them to drop in. Finally, Shirley capitulated because she had to get to a staff briefing at eight-fifteen. She was running late and didn't have time to argue.

"Go back to bed," she snapped. "I'll catch Mrs Clark before Assembly and tell her –" She didn't say, "Tell her you're faking again," but I was sure that was what she meant. When half her paperwork fell out of her briefcase as she rushed to the door, I didn't help her to pick it up. Things weren't good between Shirley and me just then.

When my sister's impatient feet had rattled away downstairs, I got back into bed and curled up under my striped duvet. I had a knot of pain below my ribs that was there all the time, but got worse when I lay sleepless, missing Mum and Dad. I felt bitter towards Shirley. She should have understood because they were her mum and dad too. But all she ever talked about was school, and what a rotten fourth-year class she had, and how much marking she had to do at the weekends.

For a while I was kept awake by the noise of car doors banging and engines starting up, but by half-past eight Goldie Court was as quiet as the grave. The only sounds were the wind blustering round the corners of the tall building and the sharp spatter of rain against the window. Sooty slid round the door and jumped up on the bed beside me. He seemed to want comfort, so I stroked him gently. His warm purring soothed me and I fell asleep.

It was nearly three o'clock when I woke again. Sooty had vanished, but as I sat up and peered at my bedside clock I could hear him mewing in another room. The apartment was quiet, and after my long rest I felt less jumpy than usual. Thinking that Sooty and I could both do with something to eat, I got up and went across the hall to the kitchen.

Sooty was on the windowsill, scrabbling at the pane and uttering uneasy little sounds. When he heard me, he leapt lightly down and rubbed himself against my legs. I poured crunchy nuggets from a packet and refilled his water bowl.

"Tuna and shrimp, your favourite," I told him, fondling his delicate ears. But Sooty didn't seem interested. As I switched on the kettle, he jumped back on the sill and began shadow-boxing in front of the glass. "What's wrong, you silly old cat?" I asked. "What can you see out there?"

Sooty said "Miaow," and tapped on the pane with his claws. Exasperated, I went to lift him down. That was when, glancing through the rain-spotted window, I saw something I'd never noticed before. On the other side of the road there was a little ornamental garden, laced with narrow paths. Neat shrubs surrounded a stone sculpture on a square plinth. Plainly it was a war memorial; the carving was of two young soldiers dressed in kilts and military tunics.

Well, fancy that, I thought, surprised rather than concerned. Since I'd lost my parents, I'd had spells of being dreamy and unobservant. Just then, however, I saw movement in the garden. A fair boy and two girls, one with dark hair and one redheaded, had come out from behind the memorial. They were older than me, probably about sixteen, and they weren't dressed for the weather. The boy was wearing a grey jacket and a blue shirt with a striped tie. The girls were in royal blue tunic dresses and pale blue blouses. Oblivious of the drenching rain and the yellow leaves flying before the wind, they sauntered through the garden. The boy was hand in hand with the dark girl, the redhead a step or two behind.

It was like watching television with the sound turned off. As the three emerged from the garden, the boy gave the dark girl a quick kiss. As they ran laughing across the road, the second girl was left alone on the pavement. As she tossed back her mane of tight red curls, her face tilted upwards. Fleetingly I saw a furious mask with compressed

6

lips and pale, flinty eyes. The apartment was warm and my shivering unexpected.

Sooty did more than shiver. With a yowl he shot off the windowsill and rocketed round the kitchen, ricochetting off the pale blue cupboards. The washing-up liquid and the toast rack went spinning. Sooty's water bowl flew into the air and there were crunchy nuggets all over the terracotta floor. I ran after him as he streaked into the sitting-room. When I caught up with him, he was writhing and spitting behind the sofa. His green eyes glared and his needle-sharp claws were extended, daring me to touch him.

"OK, please yourself," I said, backing off.

Perplexed rather than anxious, I fetched a dustpan and brush and went back into the kitchen. Sooty's nervous fits were becoming commonplace. But who were these young people, I wondered, who wandered about in summer clothes on a wet November day? It was obvious that two was company and three a crowd but, even so, the redhead's resentment seemed a bit over the top. Not, of course, that it mattered to me. I'd never seen any of them before in my life.

I spent some time sweeping up the cat food and wiping the floor. My sister was pernickety and not Sooty's greatest fan. I was putting the washing-up liquid back on the windowsill when I again glanced out into the darkening afternoon. My eyes blinked rapidly and claws sharper than Sooty's seemed to dig into my heart. The neat little garden across the road had become a jungle of grubby, unpruned shrubs – and the war memorial had disappeared.

3

A Tale of Two Sisters

It's strange how your mind tries to protect you from anything out of the ordinary. I'd spent the weeks since we moved scared to open cupboards and jumping sky-high every time the telephone rang. Yet at the first evidence that there really might be something spooky about 2 Goldie Court, I eagerly began persuading myself that there wasn't.

Of course, I assured myself as I showered and got dressed, there never had been a war memorial across the road. Perhaps a scene I'd seen somewhere else had superimposed itself on the view, like one photographic image laid on another. Perhaps, since darkness fell early in November, my eyes had been tricked by the failing light. Finally I took refuge in the most feeble cliché of all. Despite the fact that I hadn't been asleep, despite the fact that the cat had gone bananas, everything I'd seen had been a dream. Welcome to Wonderland, Alice.

Normally Shirley was home by half-past five, but I knew she'd be later tonight because there was a parents' meeting at the school. Not my year, fortunately; so far I'd been spared the humiliation of Shirley turning up as a parent to discuss my Personal and Social Development with Granny Clark. Calmed by the victory of my commonsense over wild imagination, I put a pizza in the microwave, opened a bag of cookies and made myself a big mug of coffee. While I waited for the pizza to be ready, I looked resolutely out of the kitchen window. All I saw was a tangle of shrubs in the smoky dusk, and cars slowing down at the junction of Corngate and Markethill. When the microwave pinged, I put my supper on a tray and switched on lamps in the sitting-room.

Even I had to admit that Shirley had created a cool room. I liked the pale gold carpet and the daffodil curtains. The squashy cream sofa and chairs looked good with the books, china and pictures she'd brought from our old house. But the sight of familiar objects in the wrong place still unsettled me, and sometimes I wished she'd sold the lot. Putting down my tray, I settled myself in front of the television.

I wasn't really keen on television, but it gave me an illusion of company. As I ate my pizza, I stared at a chat-show. But the voices faded and the faces became blurred as I slipped into the past, recalling this time of day when Mum and Dad were still alive.

At four-thirty, I'd just have got in from school. I'd be sitting at the pine table in our cosy, untidy kitchen, having a snack and telling Mum the news of the day. Then I'd go up to my room and do some homework, listening for Dad's car so that I could bound downstairs and give him a welcoming hug at the front door. As I relived that happy moment, all my other memories came flooding back too.

In our comfortable red sandstone house in Knightshill Avenue, we'd been an ordinary family, Mum, Dad and me – and sometimes Shirley. Because Mum had Shirley when she was twenty and me when she was thirty-four, I can't really recall my sister when she wasn't grown up. But she was the bright star I followed – beautiful, brilliant, funny, generous and kind. She left home when I was four and, through all the years when she was away at St Andrews University, I counted the days till she'd come home again. Shirley taught me to swim and to ride my bike. I climbed into her bed in the morning and told her my secrets. When I went with Mum and Dad to see her graduate with first-class Honours, it was the proudest day of my life.

I grew up round and mousy, with greenish eyes and what shampoo bottles call flyaway hair. But I loved Shirley too much to envy her rangy figure, shiny black hair and dark brown eyes. She could have had her pick of boyfriends, but the one who became her fiancé was a jerk. His name was Toby Halliday and they met at Cambridge, where Shirley had gone to study for a PhD. I suppose he was good-looking, with curly fair hair and a pleasant, blue-eyed smile. Shirley was crazy about him, but Dad said he wasn't good enough for her and he was right. After six months, the engagement was broken off. Grandma told me later that Toby Halliday had been two-timing Shirley, and had married the other woman.

I never heard Shirley mention what had happened. She didn't finish her PhD, but came back to Glasgow and moved in with friends in Woodside. She did teacher training, then commuted to a job in Millkennet, thirty miles away. I still saw her most weekends, but she wasn't the Shirley I remembered. She seemed older, moodier, less interested in me. Mum kept saying hopefully that Shirley would find a new boyfriend, but that didn't happen. Of course by that time I had a life of my own, with lots of activities and friends. Drifting away from Shirley was sad, but I could live with it. Then, one stormy January night, we were thrown back violently into each other's lives.

Grandma had come to stay with me while Mum and Dad were away in the United States for their anniversary treat. We were watching the nine o'clock news on television when we heard that the plane with their flight number had crashed into the sea. Whimpering with terror, I phoned Shirley.

"Shirley, please, please come . . ."

She was with us in less than five minutes. The three of us stood in the hall, holding one another. Grandma and I were sobbing and Shirley was trying to comfort us. She rang the airport, made tea, called the doctor to give Grandma and me sedatives, sat up alone by the phone all night.

In the nightmarish days that followed, Grandma took to her bed and I had regular fits of hysterics. Shirley took calls, answered letters and dealt with people who brought flowers. She shopped and cooked, carried cups of tea to Grandma, and slept with me so that I never had to be alone. Later, when we'd all accepted that Mum and Dad were never coming back, it was Shirley who arranged the memorial service at St Luke's. I never saw her cry, but she had a rash on her hands and dark circles round her eyes like a raccoon's.

For several weeks I felt warm and grateful to Shirley. I even began to dream of recapturing our old companionship. But no amount of gratitude could have survived the shock of what happened next.

In retrospect, I don't altogether blame Shirley. For weeks Grandma and I had let her take all the decisions, nodding like puppets and saying, "Yes, fine, Shirley. Just do what you think is best." It stands to reason she assumed we'd go along with whatever she decided to do.

When our parents' wills were read, the arrangements were so neat you'd almost have thought they expected to die before they were fifty. Shirley was to be my guardian until I grew up. The house was left to her and the money from their life insurance to me, although I'm not allowed to spend any of it until I'm eighteen. There was talk about compensation from the airline company, but that might take years – and anyway, what could compensate us?

In a way, I felt relieved. I knew I'd have cash when I needed it for University, and I assumed I'd go on living at home, with Shirley to look after me. On the night when she told me she'd bought a new apartment in Millkennet and had sold our house – my home – to her mates in Woodside, I was absolutely gutted.

"B-but why?" I stuttered, tears welling in my eyes. "Why are you doing this to me?"

Shirley didn't come and slip a comforting arm round me, as Mum always did when I started to cry. She put down her coffee mug on the kitchen table and gave it to me straight.

"Millkennet's where I earn my living, Alice. I'm sick of dicing with death on the motorway, leaving at the crack of dawn and not getting home till all hours. Now I can afford to buy a place of my own, I want it close to where I work."

I thought it was the most selfish speech I had ever heard. My tears overflowed.

"But what about me?" I wailed. "I don't want to live in Millkennet. Don't you care what happens to me?"

Shirley sighed wearily.

"I care a great deal, Alice," she said. "If I really believed you'd be better off here, I'd have planned something different. The truth is that we both need a new start, away from a house where we're constantly reminded of Mum and Dad. If we go on living here, how shall we ever escape the past?"

I wanted to scream that I didn't want to escape the past; it was all I had left. But as I looked at Shirley's pale, impassive face, I realised something as chilling as it was unexpected. I could howl until my face was blue. My reign as little queen of an indulgent adult household was over. I went on being difficult, just the same.

"I don't want to go to a school where you're a teacher. I'd be embarrassed with you around."

I knew this was offensive. Dad had been head teacher at my primary school and there had never been a problem.

13

"I expect we can ignore each other," said Shirley coldly.

"And what about Grandma?" I pressed on sullenly. "How d'you think she'll feel when she hears we're moving so far away?"

By now Shirley had had enough.

"Don't be so ridiculous, Alice," she snapped. "Of course Grandma will come with us. At her age, she shouldn't be living alone up three flights of stairs. That's why I chose an apartment with room for us all." She smiled – though not at me – as she added, "Grandma was born and brought up in Millkennet. In a way, it will be like going home."

I was still staring at the television, remembering the aftermath of these complacent words, when I heard Shirley opening the outside door.

"Hi! Sorry about this morning," she greeted me briskly, shedding her cashmere coat as she came into the sitting-room. "I meant to ring at lunchtime, but I got tied up. Are you feeling better?"

"Yeah, fine," I replied.

Shirley dropped into a chair, kicking off her cool Manolo Blahnik shoes.

"Then we really should keep our date with Grandma tomorrow," she said.

"I suppose," I muttered, my heart sinking into my pink furry slippers.

4

Poky Mansions

When I climbed into Shirley's green Renault Megane on Saturday morning, my heart was still in the region of my feet. Although I'd slept well enough, waking only twice as a train juddered by outside, I was exhausted just thinking about the day ahead.

I don't want to give the wrong impression. I love Grandma – always have, always will. But sitting for three hours in a cramped, overheated apartment, with Shirley sulking on my left and Grandma bristling on my right, wasn't my idea of chilling out on a Saturday. Shirley was to blame, but now Grandma was riling me too. Hadn't they both got what they wanted? If anyone had reason to be in the huff, it was me.

As we turned out of Goldie Court into Corngate, I couldn't resist a sideways glance at the grimy little garden. No war memorial, but then I knew that, didn't I? Sticking a Boyzone CD in the player, I lounged back in the passenger seat. Shirley isn't a Boyzone fan, but as she zipped along the bypass she managed not to wince. Steering the car confidently with her long, beautifully manicured hands, she watched the traffic and kept her thoughts to herself.

Deep down, I knew it was good of Shirley to keep me and Grandma in touch. If Grandma had laid into me the way she'd laid into Shirley, I don't think I'd ever have spoken to her again. For Grandma, it had turned out, wanted nothing less than to return "home" to Millkennet. When she heard what Shirley had been up to, she went ballistic.

"How dare you try to organise my life, you impudent squirt?" she'd bawled, wrecking what was supposed to be her sixty-fifth birthday tea. "How dare you assume that I want to be your household skivvy, and in Millkennet, of all godforsaken dumps! I hate Millkennet. Wild horses wouldn't drag me back there. Do I make myself clear?"

"Perfectly," Shirley had gulped, shivering like a net curtain in the wind.

"Good," snarled Grandma, "and do me a favour, Shirley. Remember I'm sixty-five, not a hundred and five." She chomped indignantly on a slice of birthday cake, then added triumphantly, "By the way. Last year I put my name down for one of those nice wee pensioners' flats at the top of Wistaria Avenue. I got a letter yesterday telling me one's vacant. I'm moving at the end of June."

Months later, I still couldn't help smirking at the memory of Shirley's crestfallen face. But then I too had made a mistake.

"Will you have room for me?" I asked hopefully.

Grandma saw me off as brusquely as she'd seen off Shirley.

"Certainly not," she barked. "I've better things to do than spend my old age microwaving junk food and being deafened by what you call music. You'll go with Shirley. That's what your parents wanted."

I'd still have thought it was worth a try, if I hadn't seen the wounded expression in Shirley's brown eyes. It was a sour start to our apartment-sharing, her knowing how far I'd have gone to avoid her company. Even so, Shirley reminded me to ring Grandma twice a week and, since Grandma refused to come to Millkennet even for a visit, once a month we went to lunch with her. I hated these occasions, not only because of the angry tension between two people too proud and stubborn to kiss and make up.

The other awful thing was that everywhere you looked in Grandma's living-room there was a photograph of Mum. Mum in her pram, Mum the day she started school, Mum with her sports cups, Mum getting married, Mum at Shirley's christening and many, many more. Grandma must have spent hours taking them out of photograph albums and putting them into frames. They were a painful reminder that it wasn't only Shirley and I who were bereaved. You'd only had to see them together to know that Grandma loved Mum more than anyone in the world.

Yesterday's rain had thinned to opalescent mist. The spare winter fields dropped behind on the motorway, disappearing altogether as we hit the city beyond Cumbernauld. Shirley made a detour by the University, so that we didn't have to pass our old house. When we'd parked on the forecourt of the low-rise block which Shirley called "Poky Mansions", I buzzed Grandma on the entryphone. As we went up in the lift, Shirley spoke for the first time since we'd left Millkennet.

"What d'you think it'll be today, then? Sausages and mash or mince and dumplings?"

"Steak and kidney pudding," I replied, and we sniggered in a rare moment of harmony.

In fact, it was fish pie. We could smell it even before Grandma opened the door. I said, "Hiya, Grandma," and gave her a hug. Shirley made a kissing noise some distance from Grandma's cheek and swanned into the living-room. Irritably, I watched her retreating behind the *Knightshill Courier*. Here we go again, I thought. Only this time I was wrong.

We always had lunch at a teensy table in Grandma's teensy kitchen; to call the place poky was to exaggerate its size. While we ate, Grandma asked me questions, more or less ignoring Shirley.

"Are you working hard, Alice?"

"Yes."

It was true. I had good teachers and school work helped take my mind off my troubles.

"Well, don't work too hard, will you? Do you like your new school?"

"It's OK. Modern, you know, a bit like my old one. Less graffiti, but the dinners are yuckier."

"Have you made friends?"

This was harder to answer truthfully. The kids in class 2C were OK, the normal mix of geeks and coolsters, nerdy swots and lazy prats. A few of them smoked and drank Hooch. More were health freaks who kept having to ask out to the loo because of all the bottled water they drank. They hadn't been mean to me, but Granny Clark had told them about Mum and Dad dying and they didn't know how to handle it. They didn't bully me or even shun me, but no one invited me home. When the girls arranged to go shopping on Saturday afternoon, they never asked me along.

"I know some nice kids," I'd tell Grandma evasively. "I mess around with them at break."

Today Grandma asked all the usual questions, but I sensed she wasn't paying attention to my answers. Unusually, Shirley was the focus of her dark, thoughtful gaze.

Shirley had taken about a tablespoonful of fish pie. She'd barely eaten half of it when she put her plate aside. When Grandma spoke, her tone amazed me. I hadn't heard her speak so gently to Shirley since before they'd quarrelled.

"What's wrong with you, my girl?" she asked. "You don't eat and you look so thin and ill. Does Shirley eat at home, Alice?"

Startled, I looked hard at Shirley. I'd never thought you could be too thin, probably because I have the kind of body that fattens at the sight of a jam doughnut. But Grandma was right. Shirley looked as if she hadn't slept for weeks and her cream leather jacket seemed two sizes too big.

"She doesn't eat much," I told Grandma.

"Thanks, Alice," muttered Shirley. Then she caught Grandma's eye. "It's nothing," she said. "I'm just tired.

Teaching these days isn't a bed of roses and – oh, you know how it is."

Grandma nodded sadly.

"Yes, my love, I know how it is," she said. "And I haven't helped, have I?" She didn't exactly apologise, but what she said next was a mega climb-down. "I've been thinking. Maybe it's time I came to visit you in Millkennet. I won't stay over, mind – but instead of you coming to see me next month, I'll come to see you."

I could scarcely believe my ears.

"Oh, Grandma, that'll be brilliant," I cried. "Won't it, Shirley?"

"Yes, of course." Shirley was plainly bewildered by this unexpected turnabout. "I – that is, I'll pick you up at the station, Grandma."

Grandma shook her head.

"No need for you to drive all the way to Stirling, pet," she said. "There's a bus from Glasgow every hour and I know where you live. If I get off at the Memorial in Corngate, I'll only have to cross the road."

At these words, a creepy little feeling blighted my pleasure. I waited for Shirley to say, "What memorial?" but she didn't. She just said, "Whatever you like, Grandma," and poured herself a cup of coffee. But as we left, she and Grandma hugged each other so fiercely that tears came into my eyes.

Of course, when we were back in the car, buttoned-up Shirley didn't even mention what had happened. As we sped out of Glasgow in the early dusk, I was left in silence to consider two questions. If Grandma was right about

Stirling being our nearest station, why was I disturbed every night by trains clattering by outside my bedroom window? And how could Grandma get off the bus at a war memorial I had seen, but which wasn't actually there? I didn't have answers, but I couldn't avoid one uncomfortable conclusion. I'd been in too great a hurry to dismiss what I'd seen from the kitchen window as "all a dream".

The point was underscored as soon as we got back to Goldie Court. At half-past five the pale day had already hardened into a sharp, frosty night. As I stood waiting for Shirley to fish the apartment key out of her bag, I felt my eyes drawn to the landing window. The street light was shining into the ornamental garden, bathing the sandstone soldiers in green, fluorescent light.

5

Bad Sunday

By the time I crawled shivering into bed that night, I didn't think I could possibly sleep. I'd spent the whole evening trawling between the sitting-room and the kitchen window, checking whether the war memorial was there or not. Sometimes it was and sometimes it wasn't, and I was frightened half to death. At ten o'clock, however, Shirley emerged from her study to make me a warm drink and fill a hot-water bottle, and once my light was off I crashed out cold.

The first thing I did when I got up was to hurry to the kitchen window. To my relief, there were no stone soldiers standing against the milky sky. While I ate toast and marmalade, I pondered whether to start my homework or go for a walk. Deciding that my homework would benefit if I got some fresh air first, I gulped down my coffee and pulled on my boots. When I put my head round Shirley's study door, she was already at her desk, tapping her red pen over some poor geek's English homework.

"I'm going out for a while," I said.

Shirley glanced at me over the half-moon specs that made her look like Grandma.

"OK," she said. "Will you make lunch?"

"If you'll eat it," I responded tartly.

Bounding downstairs in my blue fleece jacket, I reflected that there was at least one good thing about living in Millkennet. I was free to go out on my own. In the city there was always some story in the newspaper about a kid being mugged or abducted or run over by a truck, and parents were scared silly. Until I'd come to Millkennet I'd never gone shopping on my own, or even ridden my bike to school.

Fifty years ago, according to my History teacher Granny Clark, Millkennet had been a busy industrial town. Now all its mills and factories had closed, and it was struggling with high unemployment. But the place had a country feel, with lots of grass and open views to the river and the hills. There was no edgy feeling of danger. Shirley had quickly sussed out the only no-go area.

"There's a wood about half a mile beyond the school called the Aiken Glen. I'd rather you didn't go there."

"Why?"

"It has a bad reputation. Drug-pushing and drug-using. The police know about it, but they can't be everywhere at once."

"No problem," I agreed, since nobody minds keeping sensible rules.

As I went out through the gate, I intended to turn left, cross the railway bridge and walk briskly up Corngate towards Ingleside. This was the nicest part of Millkennet, with big old houses and lots of trees. But, just as I couldn't go into the kitchen without looking out of the window, I felt compelled to cross the road. Nervy but curious, I wandered down a damp, birch-fringed lane between the ornamental garden and the deep railway cutting. Halfway down I saw a rusty iron gate into the garden. It squeaked on its hinges as I pushed it open and went in.

The place was so overgrown, it was like a jungle. Bushes of berberis and cotoneaster choked the beds, springing across the paths and pushing up skinny shoots towards the light. I didn't like the dank November smell and I was disgusted by the litter – beer cans and plastic food containers, potato crisp bags and sodden newspaper. Still, I went on following crumbling paths towards the centre. There I found a raised stone circle, partly concealed by a drift of winter leaves.

So it *was* here, I thought, suddenly excited as I kicked the leaves aside. Underneath there was a patch of rough, discoloured cement – surely the anchor of the plinth I'd seen from the window. For all of thirty seconds I felt elated – then realised what a muggins I was. For what did my discovery prove? It had already been obvious, from Grandma's remark, that long ago there had been a war memorial opposite Goldie Court. Why it had gone was mysterious – though not half as mysterious as why I kept seeing it from our kitchen window.

I left the garden feeling cross and frustrated. I really thought the whole business was as weird as it could get. Wrong again. Walking up the lane to the road, I was alarmed to hear shrill voices on the other side of the fence. My God, there are kids on the railway, I thought in horror. Stupid little twats – do they want to be killed?

Angrily I jumped up on the fence, intending to holler at them to get off the line. But the words died in my throat, and if I made any noise it was a thin, frightened scream. There were kids all right – three of them, larking about at the bottom of the cutting near the bridge. But instead of risking death on a busy railway line, they were playing on a footpath in a quiet valley of gorse and winter grass. The railway at Millkennet had been closed and the track dismantled long ago.

I had noticed it first when Mum and Dad died. Even when you're sick with grief and fear, you can behave quite normally. As your whole life unravels, you automatically do and say ordinary things. When I got back indoors, despite my reeling head and pounding heart, I laid the table and put coffee in the percolator. I cooked pasta and opened a jar of carbonara sauce. When Shirley came to lunch, I even found something to say.

"It's cool that Grandma's going to come, isn't it?" I asked, shoving a plate in front of her.

Shirley prodded the pasta unenthusiastically with a fork.

"It would be," she agreed, "if she came. But I don't think she will."

"Why not?" I asked in astonishment. "She said she would, didn't she?"

Shirley looked unconvinced.

"On the spur of the moment," she pointed out, "because she was bothered about me."

"I'm not surprised," I said carelessly. "You look absolutely awful."

I watched Shirley biting back a snide reply.

"I was about to say," she continued coolly, "that I'm sure by now she'll be wondering how to get out of it."

"But why?" Trust Shirley, I thought indignantly, to spoil the one thing I was looking forward to. "I don't understand."

Shirley forced herself to swallow a forkful of tagliatelle. Ignoring my petulant tone, she tried to explain.

"Think how Grandma behaved the day I suggested she should come and live with us," she said. "I admit it was one of my many mistakes, but was there any need for such bluster and fury? All she had to say was, 'No, thanks.'." Shirley furrowed her dark eyebrows. "People go over the top like that when they're scared," she said.

"Scared?" I repeated incredulously. "Why on earth would she be scared?"

Shirley shrugged her narrow shoulders.

"I keep asking myself that question," she replied. "I don't have an answer. But it's what I think and I don't believe she'll come."

I could have cried with vexation. Grandma had told us back in the summer that she wouldn't be spending Christmas with us: "I just couldn't bear it," she'd said. Now, if Shirley was right, I didn't even have a pre-Christmas visit to look forward to.

"Just when I thought things were going to be OK again," I said bitterly.

"They can only improve," sighed Shirley, rising to tip most of her lunch down the waste-disposal unit.

After the morning's frightening experience, Shirley's contrariness was hard to take. When she'd taken her coffee into her study I washed up, feeling baffled and afraid. I'd have liked to get into bed and pull the duvet over my head, but I still had homework to do. I sloped into my bedroom and sat down reluctantly at my little pine desk.

Consulting my homework notebook, I decided that the most urgent task was to word-process my History project. Granny Clark was an awesome freaker if you didn't hand in work on time. But I kept pressing the wrong keys and the unforgiving blueness of the screen made my eyes ache. At twenty past two and again at ten past three, I heard a train rumble under the railway bridge.

By three-thirty I couldn't bear my overcrowded little room a moment longer. Dragging on my fleece, I bolted through the hall and down the stairs. A quick jog up one side of Corngate and down the other would clear my head, I thought. This time I wasn't tempted to go into the garden or peer down into the railway cutting. With my head down, I crossed the bridge and pounded along past garden walls overhung by ivy and unleaved trees.

Day was shutting down. By the time I crossed the road outside Millkennet High School, the air was smoky and the light almost gone. Running back over pavements glittering with frost, my body sweated but my feet tingled and my hands were like ice. I began to think longingly of wrapping my fingers round a mug of hot chocolate. As I came to the bridge I raised my head in relief, expecting to see the tall, light-studded walls of Goldie Court. What I did see made me cry out loud.

The familiar white apartment block had disappeared. In its place stood a massive building of dark grey stone. It had a high slate roof and a pillared portico. Gasping in the freezing air, I gawped at a great black door and rows of darkened windows behind high, spiked railings.

My knees felt like jelly and I could feel sickness burning in my throat. Closing my eyes, I prayed fervently that this was only a fearsome dream. When I dared to look, the grim building was gone. Lights shone serenely from Goldie Court and I could see people moving about in their kitchens, preparing their evening meals.

I forced myself to run, whimpering and scrabbling in my pocket for my keys. As I opened the outside door a chill, fetid draught blew down the stairwell. My fingers were shaking so much that I had trouble fitting the key into the apartment door. That was when I knew someone was watching me. Glancing up fearfully to the landing above, I saw a shock of bright red hair in the thin electric light. The girl I'd seen from the window on Friday was leaning over the banister. Her face was as stony and her eyes as vindictive as they'd been then. Only now they were looking at me.

6

Haunted

You don't need a big brain to work out that people seen strolling round a ghostly war memorial are likely to be ghosts. But what they had to do with me, and why I should have been singled out for persecution by the red-haired phantom were questions I couldn't begin to answer.

On each landing of Goldie Court there was a cupboard, with a chute that delivered sacks of household rubbish to a huge bin in the basement. On the evening after that dreadful Sunday, it was my turn to empty our wastepaper baskets. When I'd filled a sack, I took it out and opened the cupboard door. Instead of a brick wall a metre from my nose, I saw a long, white-tiled corridor. Sunlight shone down from high windows, making criss-cross patterns on the dusty floor. Far away I saw a small figure walking towards me. Long before the face came into focus, I recognised a blue tunic dress and a mop of frizzy red hair.

My muscles went limp and I lacked the will to turn

and run. I stood trembling with the sack in my hands but, as the ghost floated towards me, I saw that her chalk-white face was smiling. She didn't say anything out loud, but inside my head I heard a low, insistent voice. *Don't be afraid, Alice. Come with me. I want to show you something.*

She was holding out a grey, spindly hand and I was actually stepping towards her when some instinct made me glance down. At my feet there was a round hole with a steep flight of steps falling away into darkness. With a gasp of alarm, I dropped the sack and drew back into the doorway. Immediately the ghost's pleasant expression changed. Her eyes flickered and her thin mouth twisted in disappointment. As I stared, a sort of net, like thick grey cobwebs, seemed to rattle down between us. As the bricks of the wall re-formed themselves, she disappeared.

But not for long. In the days to come, she would never be far away. If I went to the door to take in a parcel, I'd see her glowering over the postman's shoulder. I'd go downstairs to fetch the milk, and she'd be watching me over the banister as I came back up. Sometimes it wasn't our banister she was leaning on. Instead of red carpeting and tubular chrome handrails, I saw worn stone steps and grim iron balustrades. The ghost didn't come close to me again, but the incident in the cupboard preyed on my mind. I dreamt of falling down holes and being pushed downstairs. I dreamt of falling from the night sky, but it was Shirley I saw drowning in the deep, dark sea.

I tried to retaliate by making faces, putting out my tongue and calling, "Yah-boo, Ginger!" It made me feel bolder, but for all the effect it had on the ghost, I might as well not have bothered. There might be a gust of tainted air, but never a blink in the cold eyes to suggest that I was bugging her at all.

I was thankful, at least, that my tormentor never appeared inside the apartment. It was bad enough there without her. The whispers and giggles that had spooked me ever since I came to Goldie Court rose in volume until the noise made me want to scream. I heard babbling voices and shrieks of laughter, which I was sure were mocking me. I began to hear music, a piano playing and a young male voice singing:

> *"Ae fond kiss and then we sever!*
> *Ae fareweel, alas, for ever!*
> *Deep in heart-wrung tears I'll pledge thee,*
> *Warring sighs and groans I'll wage thee."*

The tune echoed plaintively in my head. The poignancy of lovers' parting brought tears to my eyes.

> *"Had we never loved sae kindly,*
> *Had we never loved sae blindly,*
> *Never met – or never parted,*
> *We had ne'er been broken-hearted."*

Outside the war memorial came and went in the cold December mist – and Sooty ran away.

I suppose it was bound to happen. Sooty had always hated Goldie Court. His constant yowling and twitching had been getting on my nerves as well as Shirley's. But

31

when one morning he slipped downstairs with the paper-boy and vanished, I couldn't contain my grief. After school I ran round weeping, knocking on neighbours' doors and searching with a flashlight through other people's gardens.

"Sooty!" I sobbed. "Where are you? Sooty, please come back!"

Shirley couldn't have been kinder.

"Don't cry, honey. Cats can look after themselves. If he doesn't turn up in a couple of days, we'll put a notice in the local newspaper."

Which she did, taking time out from her mountainous paperwork to phone the notice through, and paying for it with her Amex card. But no one answered. Sooty didn't come home.

Now I couldn't bear to be alone in the apartment. I joined after-school clubs, spending two hours every day doing aerobics, playing chess, making hideous Christmas decorations for the school hall. Afterwards I waited for Shirley at the front door and got a lift home. While she spent the evening and half the night in her study, marking exam papers and writing reports, I played my CDs with the volume turned up, trying to drown the laughing and singing that beat like blows about my head. Inevitably, there were rows:

"For God's sake, Alice, turn that racket down! I can't hear myself think and the neighbours will complain."

"Oh, chut! Why can't you just leave me alone?"

Sometimes I did want to be left alone. There were also times when I wanted to throw myself into Shirley's arms and sob out my terrible story. What stopped me wasn't the fear of being laughed at – I knew Shirley better than that. She would have me taken out of school and shipped off to a child psychiatrist. There would be pills to take, and counselling sessions with some cleverclogs urging me to get in touch with my feelings about losing Mum and Dad. For who, knowing my background, would believe that my experiences were anything but the fantasies of a bereaved teenager stressed to breaking point? And God knows, I would have broken – had not someone else broken first.

7

Not Alone

"Alice," said Shirley one dark December morning, "will you do me a favour?"

It was hard to say no, because I owed her one. She'd kept renewing the notice about Sooty in the local paper, and had offered a hefty reward for his safe return.

"OK. What is it?" I inquired through a mouthful of cereal.

"Will you skip the crafts club this afternoon and come straight home?" Shirley asked. "Someone's coming at four o'clock to read the electricity meter and I have a choir rehearsal after school. I'd be really grateful."

A cold finger seemed to touch my heart, but what could I say? Apart from owing her a favour, I'd been complaining only last night that I was sick of the sight of Christmas decorations.

"No problem," I lied. "I'll be here by ten to four."

Friday wasn't my happiest school day at the best of times. The timetable was packed with my bugaboo subjects – Physics, Home Economics, French. Today it was worse than waiting to have a tooth out. I couldn't eat any lunch and I had to keep asking out of class to go to the loo. By ten to four, when I nervously let myself into Goldie Court, I'd bitten my lower lip so much that it felt bruised.

For once, however, there was no phantom on the stair. The apartment was quiet, its only sounds the fridge humming and the hot water tank saying "Gloop-gloop". I'd just taken off my jacket when a brisk young woman came and read the meter.

"Have a nice weekend," she called cheerfully, rattling away downstairs.

"Dream on," I muttered as I closed the door.

At ten past four I went to the loo, fetched a Coke from the kitchen and switched on lamps in the sitting-room. As darkness erased the trees in the park outside, I sat flicking through a magazine and tensely watching the clock. If Shirley went to the supermarket after choir practice, I calculated, she wouldn't be back much before six. So I was startled, at twenty to five, to hear the apartment door open – and a voice that wasn't Shirley's in the hall.

Jumping up, I opened the sitting-room door. To my horror I saw Granny Clark, all bony legs and big hair, with her arm round Shirley. Obviously Shirley had been crying; her eyes were red and her pale cheeks stained with tears.

"What's happened?" I gasped. "Shirley?"

Suddenly Shirley broke away from Granny Clark. Running into her bedroom, she slammed the door. Granny Clark and I peered at each other in the light from the sitting-room.

"What's happened?" I asked again.

"Shirley isn't well," Granny told me. "She's been having

35

trouble with a boy in one of her classes and today I think it just got too much for her." She glanced at her watch and gave me an anxious look. "Alice, I'm sorry," she said. "I have to go. I should have picked up my son from the swimming pool at half-past four. I'll try to call round later –"

"It's all right, Mrs Clark," I said firmly. "I can look after my sister." I saw her hesitating, so I added politely, "Thank you for bringing Shirley home. I'll phone you if we need any help."

Granny was still bobbing on the landing, saying, "Please," and "Promise," as I shut the door. Taking a deep breath, I went into Shirley's room.

Shirley had taken off her coat and dropped it on the floor. She was sitting on the side of her bed shuddering and sobbing, with her face in her hands.

"Oh, Alice," she cried. "I'm sorry. Please forgive me. I'm so sorry."

I did the only thing I could. Sitting down beside her, I put a wodge of paper handkerchiefs into her hand. Then I drew her dark head down on my shoulder and held her until she couldn't cry any more. At long last, Shirley blew her nose and dabbed at her swollen eyes.

"Forgive me," she said again.

I gave her what I hoped was a reassuring hug.

"Don't be silly," I said. "I'm going to make some tea, and then you must tell me what this is all about."

While I was in the kitchen, I heard Shirley go into the bathroom and splash water on her face. When I carried two mugs of tea into the sitting-room, she was curled up in a corner of the sofa – miserable, but at least not crying any more. As I put a mug into her hands, I noticed that the rash she'd suffered from when Mum and Dad died was back, with a vengeance.

"Right then. Spit it out," I ordered, sitting down at her side.

There was a long pause, and I had a bad moment when I thought Shirley was going to clam up on me. Then it all began to come out.

"There's a guy in my fourth-year class – Zak Petersen's his name. All this term he's been making my life hell, sneering at the books we're reading and making crass remarks to get cheap laughs from his cronies. This afternoon he was so offensive that I couldn't take any more. I reported him to my principal teacher, Mr Falconer."

I knew Mr Falconer by sight, a stiff, chalky old geezer with dry hair and a shiny suit.

"Good on you," I said emphatically.

Shirley swallowed hard and shook her head.

"It wasn't good at all," she said. "You see – nobody had told me that Mr Falconer is Zak Petersen's doting grandfather. He told me that if I couldn't enthuse a bright, eager sixteen year-old, it was time I looked for another job."

I could scarcely believe what I was hearing.

"The mean old swine," I shouted, so indignant that I spilt tea on my trousers. "I'll push his rotten teeth in!"

Shirley was usually po-faced when I criticised her nerdy colleagues, but now she smiled fleetingly. Then she said something so unexpected and chilling that I felt my whole body stiffen.

"Well, never mind. I don't suppose it matters. I shan't be there much longer."

"*Shirley?*"

"No – please, listen." She jerked her head away, avoiding my frightened eyes. "Alice, if I had to leave you for a while, would you stay with Aunt Ruth at Troon? Grandma has no room for you, and it would break my heart if you had to be fostered by strangers."

As these appalling words sank in, desolation washed over me. In that instant, where Shirley was became the only place I wanted to be. I was more terrified than when I was face to face with a ghost.

"Shirley," I whispered, "what are you saying? Where would you go?"

Shirley forced herself to look at me.

"To a hospital. I'm having a nervous breakdown," she said bleakly. "For a while I thought I might just be imagining things, but recently –"

I felt a slight prickling at the nape of my neck.

"Yes," I said encouragingly.

"I keep hearing noises," whispered Shirley, her eyes filling with tears again. "Doors banging and kids chattering and a boy singing, always the same heart-rending song. Sometimes I see a war memorial in the garden across the road. Twice I've got out of the car and – oh, God, Alice! How can I be telling you this? I've seen the school that used to be here – the one called Goldie's Academy."

The image of that grim, pillared building was clear in my mind's eye, though I'd only seen it once. It made sense that it was a school, and of course the noises I'd heard were school ones.

"Is that what it was called?" I asked gently. "The kids make a worse racket than they do at Millkennet High, don't they? Do you hear the trains too?"

I'll never forget the stunned silence, or the look my sister gave me. Anxiety, consternation and pure relief struggled for expression on her ravaged face.

"Oh, Alice!" she sighed. "You too?"

"Yes," I assured her, "and Sooty. That's why he's run away. Shirley love, if you're having a nervous breakdown, so am I. But I don't think so. This place is haunted."

Strangely, the evening that had begun with torrents of grief ended in great peace. I could see that Shirley was too exhausted to talk any more, so I did what Mum would have done. I ran her a bath, wrapped her nightie round a hot-water bottle and sent her to bed at seven o'clock. I buttered a slice of toast and boiled an egg, and took them to her on a tray.

"Eat," I ordered, and she did.

I suppose it was because she was so shattered that Shirley allowed me to boss her about but, to tell the truth, I enjoyed it. For the first time in my spoilt, babyish life, I was caring for someone whose need was greater than my own. I played Shirley one of her Bach CDs and read to her from *The Wind in the Willows*, which she used to read to me when I was a little girl. Before I went to bed, I fetched ointment from the bathroom cupboard and rubbed it gently onto her red, blistered hands.

"I'll take you to the doctor on Monday," I said.

I was serious, until I saw Shirley's lips twitch.

"Thanks, but there's no need," she said. "It's caused by stress, not leprosy, as Zak Petersen seems to think."

It was lightly said, but I knew then what Shirley's breaking-point had been.

"I'll mash that guy," I growled, "him and his mouldy old grandfather." But even as I badmouthed them, I couldn't hide from myself how much more I was to blame. I'd been foul to Shirley, venting on her the hurt we should have shared. "I'm sorry I've been such a selfish pig," I said gruffly. "When I think what you've been going through –"

Shirley would have none of it.

"Nonsense," she said. "A lot of kids in your position would have become delinquent. I'm the one who should apologise. I thought I was taking you away from a haunted house, but –" she smiled ruefully "– it seems all I've done is to bring you to live in another one."

"I'm not so frightened now that we're in it together," I told her. "Are you?"

"No. We'll talk tomorrow," Shirley said.

I was getting into bed when something odd occurred to me. When she was telling me what she'd seen, Shirley hadn't mentioned the red-haired schoolgirl. I wondered if I should mention her but, as I put out my light, I decided it would be kinder to keep schtum. If I'd seen something more than my sister had, I thought I should try to handle it on my own. You only had to look at Shirley to see she'd been frightened enough already.

8

Goldie's Academy

Unexpectedly, the peace that had descended on the apartment when I came home from school lasted. That night I slept undisturbed and woke feeling good. Shirley didn't move when I peeped round her door at eight o'clock, so I pulled on a tracksuit and ran along to the corner shop. I bought bread, milk and more eggs; Shirley hated pizza and, apart from pasta, I only knew how to cook eggs. When I got back, the phone was ringing. As I sprinted to pick it up, Shirley emerged tousled from her room.

"Hi, Grandma! You're up early," I said.

Shirley mouthed, "Don't tell her," and disappeared into the bathroom. I put down my carrier bag and took the phone into the sitting-room.

"Listen, pet," Grandma said. "Remember I said I'd come and visit you this month?"

"But you can't," I replied.

"That's right." Grandma sounded surprised that I'd got the message before it was even delivered. "I'm at Dunoon. Mary McLeod – she's the friend who asked me to stay over Christmas – thought I needed a longer break, so she

41

suggested I should come yesterday and stay till after New Year. But don't be vexed. I'll come in January, provided it doesn't snow."

"No sweat, Grandma," I said.

A sniff in Dunoon told me I wasn't sounding disappointed enough. The truth was that, with life so stressful recently, I'd practically forgotten about Grandma's visit. There was a little pause, then she said quite sharply, "That's all right, then. I've put your presents in the post."

"Thanks," I said.

Another pause, then:

"How's Shirley?"

A lie seemed in order.

"Oh, fine, I think, Grandma."

"You'll have to get her to eat, Alice."

"I'm doing my best."

"Right. I'll away then. Cheerio."

As I took the phone back into the hall, Shirley came out of the bathroom, rubbing her face on a towel.

"You were right. She isn't coming," I told her. "She even has her excuse ready for January."

Shirley made an impatient noise that sounded like, "Ach, shooch."

When she hooked the towel over her shoulder, I saw that she was shivering. Her eyes were smudgy and she was as white as a sheet.

"What's wrong? Didn't you sleep?" I asked anxiously.

"Not a lot," admitted Shirley, "though I think I could now. Do you mind if I go back to bed for a while?"

"I'll bring you a hot-water bottle," I said.

42

Shirley had said, "We'll talk tomorrow," but that didn't happen because she slept all day. Taking advantage of the blissful quiet, I stayed in my room, working on my Geography project about Canada. Grandma's younger sister, Great-aunt Alice, who lived in Toronto, had sent me a pile of brochures and postcards. As I stuck them into my folder, I felt a deep longing to see for myself the lakes, prairies and forests of that vast, beautiful land.

On Sunday morning Shirley said she'd have to write some reports. When I howled in protest she told me amiably to go jump in a pond, so I supposed she must be feeling better. After lunch we walked to Millkennet High School to pick up Shirley's car, which had been in the car park since Friday afternoon.

"It was kind of Granny Clark to bring you home," I said grudgingly.

Shirley winced.

"Alice, I do wish you wouldn't call her that," she said reprovingly. "She's only three years older than I am. I hope the kids don't call me 'Granny Fairlie'."

"They call you 'Gorgeous Fairlie'," I informed her, giggling as she blushed scarlet.

With one thing and another, it was evening before we really had time to talk. I'd made omelettes and, after we'd eaten them, we sat at the kitchen table with the fruit bowl between us.

"I've been wondering," I began, "if there is a war memorial in Millkennet."

"Yes, there is," Shirley replied. "It's in a little courtyard opposite the police station. You pass it going to the supermarket."

Which showed how observant I was.

"Is it the same one we've seen across the road?" I asked.

Shirley had to think about this. Eventually she said, "I suppose so. I've never looked closely because I have to watch the traffic at the roundabout. I intended to visit it when I first came, because Grandma's father's name must be on it, but it's difficult to park anywhere near."

I remembered Mum telling me about Grandma's father when I was learning about World War II at primary school. He'd been killed in North Africa in 1941.

"Why do you think the memorial was moved from the garden?" I asked.

Shirley paused halfway through peeling an apple.

"It may never have been there. We're talking ghosts," she reminded me.

I couldn't help feeling slightly smug.

"Yeah, but I reckon it was there," I said. "I went to look and you can still see where it was cemented down. Besides, Grandma said that if she got off the bus at the Memorial, she'd only have to cross the road."

"Did she? I don't remember that," admitted Shirley. She smiled and looked quite impressed, but then her face darkened. "Oh, Alice, I feel so bad," she said. "Why didn't you confide in me?"

"Same reason you didn't confide in me," I responded bluntly. "I didn't fancy the shrink's couch either, Shirley."

Shirley's lips twitched and I giggled, as if it was a laughing matter.

"How do you know about the school?" I asked.

"That's easy," Shirley replied. "There was a bit about it in the brochure I got when I was planning to buy this place, to explain the name 'Goldie Court'. It was a private school, opened in 1875 and called Goldie's Academy after its founder. By the early 1980s it was in financial trouble due to falling numbers, and it closed in 1986. The few remaining staff and pupils transferred to Millkennet High School."

"They wouldn't like that," I exclaimed, thinking of our sprawling modern school with its hordes of kids from all sorts of backgrounds.

"So you'd think, but apparently it worked well," Shirley said. "The teachers who came from Goldie's say that the people at Millkennet High went to endless trouble to make everyone feel welcome. They even insisted on displaying Goldie's trophies and dux boards in the hall beside their own."

Needless to say, I hadn't noticed these either.

"What kind of ducks?" I inquired. "Are they painted ones?"

Shirley gave me a pained, teacherly look.

"Dux is a Latin word, spelt d-u-x, meaning 'leader'," she explained Granny Clarkishly. "The dux of a school was the pupil with the best overall marks in the final year."

"Thank you, Miss Fairlie," I said ironically. "Do you suppose Grandma went to Goldie's Academy?"

Shirley raised incredulous eyebrows.

"Sometimes, when I listen to her conversation, I

wonder if Grandma went to school at all," she said. "But no, she couldn't have. Goldie's charged fees and Grandma's family was very poor."

I knew this was true. Grandma had worked as a nursemaid in a big house when Mum was a little girl.

"So, what happened to the building?" I asked.

"What usually happens," said Shirley. "It stood empty, was vandalised and became derelict. About four years ago it was demolished."

"And now it's come back to haunt us," I said, mystified. "A school that closed before I was born. We can even hear trains running past it on a non-existent line. But why?"

Shirley spread her palms in a helpless gesture.

"My love, I don't know," she said.

I was packing my bag for school when something else occurred to me. When I heard Shirley coming out of the bathroom, I went into the hall.

"Just one thing," I said. "Do you think the other people who live in these apartments are haunted too?"

Shirley tossed back her wet hair and looked at me with thoughtful eyes.

"Good question," she said, "but no. If the haunting were general, I expect we'd have had an angry residents' meeting about it by now. Something unnatural has been unleashed here. I haven't a clue why, but I'm sure it only concerns you and me."

9

End of Term

When Shirley had mentioned his name, I'd known at once who she was talking about. Zak Petersen would have stood out in any crowd. It wasn't just that he was tall and snake-hipped, with dyed blond hair and piercing, pale blue eyes. It wasn't even that he seemed to find Millkennet High School a bad smell under his long nose. It was his gear that set him apart.

Millkennet High was keen for everyone to wear the school uniform. It was comfortable, if not cool; a dark blue sweatshirt with grey trousers or skirt and an optional blue blazer. Most people wore bits of it, but not Zak Petersen. Like a peacock in a hen run, he strutted in a posh black leather jacket and cashmere rollneck. His fine tweed trousers were pure designer chic. He was wicked, from the gold ring in his ear to the soles of his expensive leather boots.

Zak Petersen wasn't a gang leader. He was far too individual for that. But guys like him attract hangers-on. Because the fifth and sixth-years had their own common-rooms, the fourth-years were kingpins in the vestibule where we sheltered in bad weather. The warmest corner, naturally, was reserved for Zak Petersen. There he lolled, surrounded by the handful of would-be tough guys and pathetic prats who admired his gear, sniggered at his smart remarks and queued for him at the tuck shop to buy his Diet Coke. The girls were worse than the boys:

"Ooh, like your sweater, Zak!"

"Cool watch. Is it a real Rolex?"

I had always despised these fawning idiots, but that hadn't stopped me thinking that Zak Petersen was a cool guy.

Now, of course, my opinion had changed. All weekend I'd been fantasising about cutting the sleeves off his cashmere sweater, filling his fancy boots with mud and dropping his Rolex down a drain. Only on Monday morning, when I saw Shirley's strained, apprehensive face, I realised that vengeful imagining might not be enough.

"Go back to bed," I pleaded. "Even you are allowed a day off. I'll go and tell old Falconer that you've got green monkey disease."

This feeble attempt at wit fell flat.

"Alice," Shirley said, "don't tempt me. If I don't go back to work today, I don't think I'll ever go back at all."

These were frightening words.

I had Biology and Geography before break. Although I liked both these subjects, I just couldn't concentrate. While the teachers banged on, I sat staring out of the window into grey, whirling sleet. Was Shirley going to have a nervous breakdown after all? Would I end up lodging with grouchy Aunt Ruth at Troon? No way, I told myself grimly. But what was I to do? Having a word in Zak Petersen's gold-ringed ear seemed as far-fetched as spilling the beans to the headmaster. When the break bell rang, I wandered disconsolately into the corridor. Unresisting, I was pushed along in the rush to the tuck shop.

As I came through the swing door into the vestibule, I saw Zak Petersen. Someone had left the outside doors wide open, and a coating of dirty slush had been blown in onto the tiled floor. With his hands in his pockets, he was casually kicking the slush into the faces of kids in the tuck shop queue. At the sight of him, something inside me snapped. Throwing down my book bag, I stalked up to him and grabbed him by the lapel.

"Stop that, you mean pig," I shouted in his face, "and listen to me!"

I don't think I've ever seen anyone so amazed. Brushing my hand disdainfully off his jacket, he peered at me as if I was some disease-carrying fly.

"Who the hell are you?" he said.

I was aware of a crowd gathering. I could hear gasps of excitement as geeks and coolsters jostled for a good view. But this was personal. I glared into Zak Petersen's pale, resentful eyes.

"Alice Fairlie," I said. "My sister is your English teacher and I'm sick of you making her life hell. Her mum and dad were killed in a plane crash in January. She isn't well and the last thing she needs is a big oaf like you giving her grief. So leave her alone, OK?"

There was a thrilled silence. I could almost hear the

spectators licking their lips. I didn't expect Zak Petersen to hit me. Physical bullying is usually single-sex. But I did expect a stream of verbal abuse and braced myself for it. Only he didn't say anything at all. For a long moment he stared at me, a tiny frown breaking the ivory smoothness of his face. Then he just walked away. With an audible breathing-out of disappointment, the crowd parted to let him through.

When I went into my History class, opinion about me was clearly divided. There was a scatter of applause and one or two people called out, "Good on you, Alice," and, "Well done!"

Others were unimpressed.

"Your mouth's too big, Alice."

"You'll be sorry you took on that guy."

As if I cared. It was almost the end of the period when the real enormity of what I'd done overwhelmed me. When Shirley hears about this, I thought, she'll kill me.

I didn't set eyes on Shirley until five o'clock. True to her long-ago promise to ignore me in school, she walked straight past me in the hall. I had to scurry after her as she clipped down the steps to the car park in her high heels. I was still fumbling with my seat belt when she flicked on the lights and drove out onto the road. Still nothing was said. We were in the sitting-room when Shirley threw down her belongings and fixed me with black, unsmiling eyes.

"Alice," she said sharply, "what did you say to Zak Petersen today?"

Oh, chut, I thought. I've gone and made things worse. Still, I didn't feel like cowering.

"Who says I said anything?" I hedged.

"He does." Shirley sat down suddenly on the sofa, as if her knees felt weak. "It was extraordinary. He sat like a lamb through my class, and then he stayed behind and apologised. He said he never meant to upset me – he just thought he was geeing the class up a bit. When you told him I was having a bad time, he realised he'd been over the top."

This was infuriating.

"If you know, why ask?" I demanded indignantly. "What's your problem?"

Shirley pushed her hair out of her eyes and looked at me more gently.

"I have problems, all right," she said. "One – at my age I shouldn't need my little sister to fight my battles for me. Two – if that boy had reacted differently, you'd have made an enemy away out of your league. Three – well, it's fishy."

"How so?"

"It's so unlike him. I wonder what he's really up to?"

"It might be true," I suggested. "Maybe he has a conscience."

"Maybe pigs can fly," retorted Shirley.

We had a pleasant evening, all the same. Since neither of us could face another egg, Shirley phoned for a Chinese takeaway. We shared satay chicken and vegetable chow mein in front of the television then, since Shirley had finished her reports, she cleared up while I did some homework. By the time I was through, she was in bed.

"Have you noticed?" I asked, when I went in to say

good night. "There haven't been any weird noises since Thursday. Maybe the spook school's having a holiday."

"Let's hope it's a long one." Shirley yawned, pulling up her duvet. "Make sure I locked the door, Alice."

"OK. Shirley –"

"What?"

"Are you cross with me?"

"No. I'm grateful. Thanks."

I'd been dreading Christmas since last January. Now, as lighted trees appeared in the windows of Corngate and carols rang out from the school music rooms, I tried desperately but in vain to block out my memories. Dad up a ladder in the hall, putting the star on top of our red and gold tree; my stocking, always filled by Shirley, on Christmas morning; Grandma coming up the path with her bag of presents; Mum and Shirley drinking sherry and getting giggly in the kitchen before lunch. This year, Grandma hadn't been able to face Christmas with the remnant of her family. I couldn't face the junior school disco, or the carol concert, or the relentless merriment of the sixth-year pantomime. Shirley was understanding.

"I'll arrange for you to go to the Clarks," she said. "Dorothy –" that was what Shirley called Granny "– has little kids who'll amuse you. I'm afraid I have to go and be merry at school – it's my job."

However, when Shirley went to ask Mr Croy, the headmaster, to excuse me, he insisted on excusing her as well.

"We all know how painful this Christmas must be

for you and Alice. Next year will be better," he said kindly.

I didn't believe this, nor I think, did Shirley. But we were grateful for a few quiet, ghost-free evenings, and two good things that happened at the end of term. The first was that Mr Falconer apologised to Shirley.

"I was out of order, Miss Fairlie," he said, in his stuffy way. "I have spoken to Zak and he has promised to behave well in future. I hope you will forgive us both."

"What a silly old windbag," I said impatiently, when Shirley told me.

Shirley shook her head seriously.

"He's a strange, sad man," she said. "His wife died in the summer and he seems completely wrecked."

The second good thing was that, on the last day, I got a truly awesome report. In spite of my absences, I got a Band 1 for everything except Home Economics. All my teachers said nice things about me, even Granny Clark.

"Alice is a pleasant, co-operative pupil," Granny had written. "She enjoys History and, with recent improved attendance, shows much promise."

Inaccurate, but who was complaining?

My guardian, "Miss Fairlie", was out of her head with delight. Although she didn't say so, I reckoned she was also gobsmacked. Shirley had gone to Hutcheson's Grammar School on a scholarship, but no one had ever thought of me as an academic high-flier. Now she had the air of someone whose goose has magically turned into a swan. In the evening, she took me to Jake's Bistro for a celebration supper.

"Shall I make a copy of the report for you to send to Grandma?" she asked, making me choke on my mushroom risotto.

"For a laugh, you mean?" I giggled. It was a family joke that when Grandma asked if you were working hard at school, she was running out of conversation. "'Happiness is more important than top marks, David.'," I quoted, remembering Dad freaking out every time she'd said it.

Shirley grinned reminiscently. The spectacle of her father going into orbit had been one of her great joys.

"Let's send the report anyway," she said. "Everyone likes their kids to do well at school."

10

Not Like Christmas

Back in the summer, when Grandma had announced that she wouldn't spend Christmas with us, Shirley had asked me what I thought we two might do. Oozing charm, I told her exactly what I thought:

"You can stuff Christmas in the dustbin, for all I care. I hate Christmas. I don't ever want it to be Christmas again."

"I only wondered if you'd prefer to stay at home or go away," Shirley had said mildly.

"Home?" I sneered. "What home?" But even at my most poisonous moments, the hurt in her brown eyes could pierce me like a needle. "Oh, do what you like," I growled. "What does it matter?"

So once more Shirley coped alone. In September she booked a chalet in the grounds of a hotel and country club overlooking Loch Lomond. She left the brochure describing the swimming-pool, gym and squash courts on the kitchen table. I tore it up and put it in the bin. Christmas wasn't mentioned again.

I couldn't have imagined then how glad I'd be, on Christmas Eve, to help load our suitcases, sports gear, CD player and food hamper into the car. As we drove from Millkennet towards the Highland Road, I felt almost light-hearted.

"Fancy a blast of Oasis?" I asked teasingly.

"Oh, please! I'd love it," Shirley groaned.

It wasn't like Christmas, but that was the idea. On Christmas morning, we opened the envelope Grandma had sent and found two book tokens. I gave Shirley a bottle of *Acqua di Giò*, and she gave me a basket crammed with goodies from Clinique and Space NK.

"To save you the trouble of nicking mine," she said.

We spent the rest of the holiday swimming and playing hard games of squash. When it wasn't raining we walked by the loch, breathing the brackeny air and skimming flat stones across the indigo water. In the evenings, we escaped from the lights and laughter of the hotel to the shelter of our little chalet. We drank some white wine and had delicious things to eat from Shirley's hamper. I can't say we never cried, but we stopped being ashamed to cry in front of each other. We also began to talk naturally about the past, and let Mum and Dad come back into our lives.

"Shirley, what was it like before I was born?"

"History."

"No, honestly?"

"It was horrible. I hated being an only child. So much anxiety and expectation, all concentrated on me. Getting a scholarship, winning prizes, pleasing my parents – I was old before my time."

"Is that why Grandma's against education?"

"She isn't against it, exactly. She doesn't understand its importance because she's uneducated herself. But she certainly thought Mum and Dad leant on me too hard. Then you came along and everyone relaxed."

"You didn't think I was a cuckoo in your nest?"

Shirley looked amazed.

"Of course not. My problem was being loved exclusively. Having you gave Mum and Dad a new focus. The pressure came off me to be a perfect only daughter." She smiled and added, "Besides, you were sweet. My only regret is that I had to go away to University when you were so small. I used to count the days till I could get home and see you again."

I remembered how I had counted the days too.

"Do you –" I said, "I mean, can you still like me, after –"

A cushion came flying across the room and thwacked me in the stomach. It was the only answer I ever got. The lesson I learned that evening was that you can love people deeply without thinking them perfect in every way.

After lunch on the third day of a new year, we packed the car and drove back down the loch side. In thin sunshine that shyly hinted at spring, we stopped near Arden for a final view. At first we sat in silence, watching the winter sun tinting the mountain landscape scarlet, coral and pink. We hadn't spoken at all of the haunted place we were returning to, but eventually Shirley said, "Alice, I need to ask you about something."

"What?"

"About moving from Goldie Court."

"Are we moving?"

"Yes, of course. We can't go on living indefinitely in a haunted house. My problem is that I have so much to do next term. All my senior classes have exams in January, then I have to produce the sixth-year play and rehearse my choir for the music festival. In March there are junior school assessments. I don't think I can find time to organise a removal. If you could hold on until Easter, I'd put the apartment on the market and rent a place for the summer term."

"And then?"

"I'm not sure. My prospects at Millkennet High will be clearer by the middle of next term. But I promise that whatever we do in the future, we'll decide together."

I thought for a moment, then I said, "I can stand it till Easter, if you can. The racket's a nuisance, but it isn't as if we've been injured or anything. Besides, it was very quiet before we left, wasn't it? Maybe the spooks have gone away for good."

Shirley gave me one of her dark, pensive looks.

"Somehow, that would surprise me." Switching on the engine, she looked in her mirror and backed out onto the road. "Anyway, thanks, Mousie," she said.

I couldn't help laughing. Nobody had called me "Mousie" since Mum had put her foot down about it when I was seven. As we sped along the dark road home, however, I was uneasily aware that I hadn't been candid with Shirley. I had never told her about the young lovers

I'd once seen in the memorial garden, or about the jealous schoolgirl who haunted Goldie Court.

The question of why only I saw the ghost didn't trouble me; I supposed I was just more sensitive than Shirley. Yet I was sure that if she knew there was an actual phantom around who'd taken a dislike to me, she wouldn't be talking about staying until Easter. But I still didn't tell her. She was looking so much better after her holiday; I dreaded seeing a haunted, prematurely old expression on her face again. As long as the ghost didn't appear inside the apartment, I reckoned I could manage her.

As if to prove finally that only I could see her, the ghost was waiting at Goldie Court. As we were humping our belongings upstairs, a familiar draught spiralled downwards. Looking up, I saw the redhead standing outside our neighbour's door. Although her cold, seagull's eyes were fixed on Shirley, Shirley walked straight past her.

"Lord, it's cold, Alice," she said, shivering as she bent to pick up the scatter of mail in the hall. "I'm glad we left the central heating on."

I felt so cocky that I did something unwise – and was immediately punished. Sticking out my tongue at the ghost, I said, "Happy New Year, Ginger!" Then I jumped into the hall and banged the door behind me. Instantly the doorbell rang. I got such a fright that I dropped everything, shot into the bathroom and locked myself in. Only when I heard Shirley talking cheerfully to the caller did I open the door a slit and peep out. On the doormat I could see our neighbour, Mrs Huntly, and –

"Sooty!" I screamed, running to embrace my cat, who was coiled round Shirley's elegant ankles. "Oh, you bad animal! Where have you been?"

"He was scratching round your door this morning," Mrs Huntly told us. "I took him in and fed him with my own cat. I'm sure he'll be pleased to see you home."

Well – yes and no. Sleek, well-nourished and smug, Sooty was pleased to see one of us home. Annoyingly, it wasn't me. Shirley wasn't a cat-lover, and she only put up with Sooty because he was mine. He'd never bothered her before because he didn't like her either. Yet now it was her legs he kept rubbing himself round, waving his tail and uttering affectionate little cries.

"Get him off, Alice," ordered Shirley, not at all amused.

I wasn't amused either. As I lifted Sooty, he squirmed out of my arms and ran after Shirley into her bedroom. Jumping onto the bed, he purred triumphantly, stretching out his legs and tail. When Shirley indignantly yanked the duvet and tipped him off, he ran round the end of the bed and lovingly ripped her tights. Eventually we had to shut him in the kitchen, where he yowled piteously.

"I wonder who's been looking after him all these weeks," mused Shirley.

"Why?"

"Maybe they'd take him back," she said sourly.

11

A Storm in January

It would be wonderful to report that Shirley and I lived in harmony ever after. Wonderful but, sadly, untrue. It wasn't my nicking her posh tights that caused friction, or even Sooty's sudden passion for her white duvet. The beginning of the spring term brought a new, completely unexpected discord.

Although the feeling made me ashamed, I was secretly glad to go back to school. In the few remaining days of the holiday, Shirley had put herself out to entertain me. She'd taken me to the cinema and the squash courts at Stirling University. On the last day we'd gone to Edinburgh, where she bought me a new fleece at Gap and a pair of Timberland boots. I'd wanted her to buy a dress, but she wouldn't. Although her clothes were as cool as Zak Petersen's, Shirley didn't have a packed wardrobe; she believed in saving for the best she could afford.

"I need shoes," she said. "I'll buy some when we go to London."

"Are we going to London?" I asked eagerly.

"Yes. I thought we might have a little jaunt in the spring," said Shirley, "to celebrate our escape from Ghostie Court."

It was laughing at jokes like this that kept us going. Since our return from Loch Lomond, the invisible school children had been out in force. We were constantly disturbed by banging doors, a thumping piano and a cacophony of talk we couldn't decipher. Whenever I opened the apartment door, I saw the ghost glowering. I had nightmares of falling down dark stairs and, just before impact, seeing Shirley sprawled beneath me. It seemed a very long time until Easter.

As I ironed my uniform the night before school began, I felt angry and frustrated because I still hadn't a clue why any of this was happening. I had no idea who the red-haired girl was, or why she'd chosen me to persecute. As for the two young people whose love she'd envied, I'd only glimpsed them once through pouring rain and had no memory of their faces. I went to bed eager for school and a break from interminable, unanswerable questions.

The first day back was clear and mild, following a night of heavy rain. There was the cheerfulness you always get in a school at the start of a new term, when your hockey boots are clean, your teachers in a good mood and no one has yet mentioned the dreaded word, "Assessments". After lunch I was chilling out on the steps with Gillian and Louise, the nearest I had to mates in my class. Looking up from *Adrian Mole: the Cappuccino Years*, bought with Grandma's book token, I saw Zak Petersen coming in my direction. Four hangers-on minced behind him, like cheesy bridesmaids following a bride.

Commonsense suggested I should scarper, but pride prevented me. I put the book in my pocket and tried to look unconcerned. To my amazement, Zak gave me a friendly wave and ordered his retinue to get lost.

"Hi, Alice. Happy New Year! Fancy a walk?" he said.

My response might have been more laid-back, I suppose.

"Who? Me?" I squealed.

Zak grinned.

"Yeah, if you like," he said.

Trying not to do a fish-on-dry-land impersonation, I got to my feet. Under the incredulous gaze of those who, not long ago, had heard me bawling him out in the vestibule, I strolled with Zak across the courtyard. Skirting the muddy playing field, we reached the fence where the school grounds met the back gardens in High School Drive. Zak lounged on the fence, looking me over with his pale blue eyes.

"Hey, I'm really sorry," he said. "I honestly had no idea I was upsetting Miss Fairlie. She never once showed. I thought –"

"You were geeing the class up," I interrupted. "She told me. But –"

"What?"

"You shouldn't have said what you did about her hands," I burst out angrily. "The rash comes when she's stressed out. It was a cruel thing to say."

Zak hunched his shoulders and hissed through his teeth. He looked genuinely ashamed.

"I do feel bad about that," he said, "but she was

bugging me that day. First she wouldn't let me read a decent part in *Romeo and Juliet*, then she ignored me the whole period. I like her to pay me attention," he confessed with a wry smile. "Has she forgiven me?"

"She forgives everyone," I said.

"Cool," said Zak. "My New Year resolution, to be a good boy – in my English class."

The bell for afternoon school shrilled across our conversation. As we walked back, I wondered what this had all been about. Zak had already apologised to Shirley, so why did he want to talk about their misunderstanding with me? And why did I feel so disappointed that that was what he wanted to talk about? His parting words left me thunderstruck.

"This is Thursday, isn't it? Tomorrow at lunchtime I have a music lesson. Maybe I'll see you at the weekend?"

Before I had time to respond, he sprang lightly up the steps and disappeared.

News doesn't half get around. Perhaps Shirley was looking out of the staff-room window. Perhaps Granny Clark was, and thought that her Personal and Social Development portfolio gave her the right to snitch to Shirley about my Personal and Social Development. Whatever the truth, I hardly had time to put down my bag that evening before Shirley freaked.

"Alice, I don't want you hanging around with Zak Petersen," she screeched, scowling like Grandma.

"Oh, chut! I thought you wanted me to make friends," I scowled back.

"Don't be ridiculous. Of course I want you to make friends. You're with me far too much and it worries me. But Zak Petersen isn't a suitable friend for you."

"Why not?" I was bawling now. "He apologised, didn't he?"

Shirley bared her teeth and brought down her clenched fist on the kitchen table.

"Apologised? Too right! And now we know why, don't we? The sneaky little toad fancies *you*." I couldn't help a wee smirk, which she saw. "I won't have it," she snarled. "He's three years older than you and he's a bad lot, Alice. He has some very shady friends and there's a strong rumour that he's involved in this Aiken Glen business –"

I knew what that meant and I was outraged.

"I'd never touch drugs," I said indignantly. "You don't have to worry about *that*, Shirley."

An ugly flush rose on Shirley's pale face.

"Believe me, that's not all I'm worried about," she retorted bitterly. "You're not to speak to him again. I absolutely forbid it."

I could hardly believe what I was hearing. This was worse than being an ogre's child.

"Shirley," I hollered, "just cool it, will you? I love you, but you can't choose my friends."

There was a moment's silence, when you could almost see the fear and hostility sizzling between us. Then Shirley backed off. Sitting down at the table, she ran her fingers distractedly through her hair.

"You're right, Alice," she said quietly. "I can't choose your friends and if you choose unwisely I can't protect you. But – oh, my dear, you're so young and so pretty, and I want everything to be good for you. I ruined my own life with one terrible misjudgment, and I was years older than you are. Promise me you'll be careful."

This was heartrending. In four years, Shirley had never mentioned Toby Halliday to me. At the age of nine I'd had a primitive desire to kill him, but it had never occurred to me that Shirley still saw her life as ruined. I felt so sorry for her, I wanted to put my arms round her and promise I'd never go near Zak Petersen again.

But I couldn't. Giving in would give Shirley power over me that I honestly didn't think she should have. Besides, Zak was too cool to give up. I'd revelled in the awed looks of the other girls as he'd walked with me across the courtyard. The idea that he liked me was flattering and exciting.

"Trust me. I promise I'll be careful," was all I could say.

"Right." Shirley rose abruptly. "I have to write up my plan of work tonight. Will you bring me some coffee later?"

"And a sandwich," I said. "Grandma says I have to get you to eat."

"Dear God," sobbed Shirley, leaving the kitchen with her briefcase under her arm.

Later that evening, after I'd done some Maths and had a shower, I sat on a stool in front of my dressing-table. Thoughtfully, I examined my reflection in the mirror. When Shirley had said earlier that I was pretty, I'd been surprised. When I was little, everyone had called me

"Mousie", and that was how I'd seen myself. Even now, I reckoned that my chin was too round and my nose too pointed to be beautiful. I was also a tad overweight.

On the brighter side, my light-brown hair had thickened since Shirley started taking me to a good hairdresser. My eyes were an unusual shade of green and I had no spots. I went to bed feeling quite positive about myself.

12

Zak's Den

I had gone head to head with Shirley on Thursday evening. By Saturday lunchtime I was in despair. I'd hung around all day at school on Friday, waiting for Zak to get in touch about meeting at the weekend. Then I'd spent the whole evening prancing to the phone, taking calls from double-glazing companies, Glasgow friends of Shirley's, an old wifie who thought we were Sam's Taxi, and Granny Clark. When Zak hadn't made contact by eleven, I'd gone bitterly to bed.

Saturday morning was our time for household chores. While Shirley, who had developed a dreadful cold, cleaned the kitchen, I scooted round with the Hoover. Its wailing drowned out the noise of Goldie's Academy, which didn't recognise weekends. It also covered the painful silence that had again fallen between Shirley and me. When I thought how I'd broken my fragile friendship with my sister in the hope of dating an unreliable prat, I could have wept.

By half-past one Shirley had shut herself in her study.

I was lounging in the sitting-room, watching football on TV, when someone pressed the buzzer downstairs. Jehovah's Witnesses, I thought irritably. Saturday was their day. Grabbing the handset in the hall, I opened my mouth to tell them to push off. I was stunned when a voice said, "Hi, there! It's Zak. May I come up?"

"OK," I squeaked.

I hardly had time to run a comb through my hair before the bell on the landing pinged. When I opened the door, Zak was on the doormat. He was wearing his leather jacket and trademark rollneck in ice blue, with expensive trainers and achingly slim black denim jeans. I was ashamed of the limp cords and baggy T-shirt I'd put on to clean the floors.

"Yoo hoo," grinned Zak. "Am I allowed in?"

"Um, yeah," I said, with a fearful glance at the study door. As Zak stepped into the hall, it opened and Shirley looked out. Her expression would have soured cream.

"What on earth do you want?" she said.

Actually, Shirley wasn't looking her best either. She was dressed in an old pair of Levis and a tatty pink shirt knotted carelessly around her midriff. She had no make-up on, her hair was a mess and her granny reading glasses had slipped half way down her inflamed nose. Zak gave her a friendly smile.

"I'm sorry to be a nuisance, Miss Fairlie," he said. "I came about that book you recommended to us on Thursday, A Guide to Postmodernism. I've been to the library, but they don't have a copy. I wondered if I might borrow yours."

Smart thinking, I thought, trying not to laugh. Shirley didn't bat an eyelid.

"Of course. I'll fetch it."

"And I'll make Zak a coffee," I said.

I was in the kitchen when Shirley returned with the book. I strained my ears to hear the conversation, which was brief.

"You have a bad cold, Miss Fairlie."

"That's an understatement, Zak."

"Shame. Will you be joining us for coffee?"

"I'm afraid not. I have a lot to do."

"Well, thanks for the book. You've got me interested in Po-mo. See you on Monday."

When I took the coffee into the sitting-room, Zak was prowling around, looking at things. His deafness to the noise of Goldie's Academy spooked me; I still found it disturbing that such an uproar was audible only to Shirley and me.

"Cool room," approved Zak, admiring some Japanese prints and running his finger along a shelf of CDs. They weren't my Boyzone and Oasis recordings, but Shirley's nerdy Delius, Mahler and Kurt Weill. "Great music," he enthused, accepting a coffee mug.

I goggled in disbelief.

"You like that stuff?"

Zak nodded.

"And some. I'm doing Higher Music next year – piano and bassoon – and I sing a bit. Hey, here's some John Tavener. Cool." I was still gaping when he stuck Shirley's book in his pocket and downed his coffee like a glass of beer. "Do you want to go out?" he asked.

Did I want to go out? I practically tripped myself rushing to put on my new black fleece and Timberland boots. As we walked out into the cold, clear afternoon, I could have shouted with joy. At last, my dream of Zak taking me to Cavelli's Café, where the cool set from Millkennet High hung out on Saturdays, was about to come true. What he actually suggested took me completely by surprise.

"Let's go to my place and have another coffee. I'd like to show you my den."

I had an inconvenient vision of Shirley's horrified face.

"Oh – um, well – is your mum in?" I mumbled.

"Eh?" Zak looked vaguely surprised. "Yeah, she is, as a matter of fact. She's on call, but so far today babies are popping normally."

What was I to do? Refusing would make me look ridiculous, as well as being sudden death to our friendship. So I nodded agreement. As we walked along Markethill, I assured myself that Mum wouldn't have minded, provided Dr Petersen was at home.

The Petersens lived in the top two floors of a large house in Church Terrace, five minutes' walk from Goldie Court. Zak took me in at a side door and led me up a green-carpeted stair. At the top was a square hall with flower paintings, pot plants and white panelled doors. Zak opened one, revealing a steep, narrow stairway.

"You go on up. I'll make the coffee," he said.

The little stair opened straight into a huge attic room with coombed walls painted blue. A huge window provided a wonderful view over purple slate roofs to the slinky grey river. I saw posters for Scottish Opera, crammed bookshelves, a black leather sofa and a lovely carved wooden elephant on a shelf.

What made Zak's den unusual, however, was the amount of wickedly expensive equipment it contained. There was a vast hi-fi system in an alcove, flanked by shelves containing hundreds of CDs. There was a state-of-the-art computer and printer, a wide-screen television and video-recorder, a keyboard, a drum kit, a camcorder and a cabinet full of computer games. I reckoned the lot must be worth thousands of pounds. I knew Zak's mum was a hospital doctor, but even so . . .

"Nice place. Your mum and dad are very good to you," I said, sitting down on the sofa as Zak appeared, carrying two metallic coffee mugs on a perspex tray.

"My dad works in Kuwait," he said, putting the tray down on a glass-topped table. "We don't see much of him but, yeah, his cheques are very generous. And of course I have my wages as a cleaner."

"Eh?" I said.

Zak handed me a mug, switched on a lamp and sat down at the other end of the sofa. Crossing his long legs, he grinned at me across an expanse of black leather.

"You'd never have guessed I was a Mr Mop, would you?" he teased. "Well, I am. Every Saturday morning I pack my apron and rubber gloves and go to my granddad's place. He's the world's best reason for teaching boys Home Economics."

"Why?"

"Because the old fool doesn't know what a duster's for," replied Zak impatiently. "Since my gran died in August, his house is like a bombsite. I'm his home help. Sweated labour at four pounds an hour."

I remembered Shirley telling me that Mr Falconer's wife had died in the summer.

"I'm sorry about your gran," I said politely. "Did she die suddenly?"

"Yip," said Zak. "She had heart trouble, but no one thought it was serious till she fell down in the kitchen with the dishtowel in her hand. Mum thought the old guy would perk up quite quickly – Gran wasn't an easy woman to live with. Instead he went to pieces. Now he just sits in the mess, grizzling and dreaming of bygone days. God knows what he'll do when he retires."

"Is he going to?"

I tried not to sound too eager, but I couldn't help thinking this would be good news for Shirley. I felt sorry for Mr Falconer but, after what he'd said to her, he'd never be flavour of the month with me.

"At Easter," Zak replied. "He'll be sixty-five on All Fools' Day. Believe me, it can't come soon enough."

"How so?"

"Get real," groaned Zak. "How am I supposed to keep a cool profile at school with my granddad breathing down my neck all the time?"

It seemed to me he managed nicely, but I let it pass.

"I thought it might be like that with Shirley," I admitted, "but it's worked out OK."

"That's different," Zak said. "It would be cool being

related to Miss Fairlie. She's a class act. Old Falc's just a sad act."

I couldn't pretend otherwise. There was silence while I drank my coffee and wondered what was going to happen next. Out of the side of my eye, I saw Zak put down his mug, unwind his legs and slide his bottom across the shiny leather space between us. A little shiver ran through me as I looked at his thigh, slim but muscular under his denim jeans. I drew in my breath as he leaned forward . . . and picked up a couple of brochures from the table.

"Come on, help me," he said. "My Granddad's giving me a motorbike for my seventeenth birthday. I can't decide whether to have a Yamaha YZF-RI or a Kawazaki ZX-9R. Or should I go for something retro?"

Of course, I feigned interest, but enthusing about titanium silencers, gearshifts and magnesium engine covers didn't come easily to me. About three-fifteen the telephone rang downstairs. It was picked up immediately, and a moment later a woman's voice called, "Zak! I have to go out. Get yourself a takeaway if I'm late."

Zak got up and sloped to the top of the stair.

"OK, Ma. I'm just going out myself. See you sometime."

Five minutes later, I parted from Zak on the pavement outside his house. He was in a hurry, because he had to meet a guy down town at half-past three.

"Nice seeing you, Alice," he said, hopping onto his mountain bike.

He rode off without even kissing me goodbye.

13

Girls and Boys

You would think that, if you were haunted, you'd feel too spooked to worry about ordinary things. That was how I'd been at the beginning, goggling and hyperventilating like Sooty without fur. Eventually, though, I'd achieved a kind of balance, so that my ghostly experiences didn't entirely dominate my everyday life. It was just as well, since two days after my visit to Zak's den, my haunting moved into a new phase.

Overnight on Saturday, Shirley's cold had got even worse. She sneezed all day on Sunday and, during the night, ghost trains outside and coughing through the wall almost drove me crazy. On Monday at lunchtime, a sixth-year girl brought me a note in Shirley's spidery handwriting: *Alice, have cancelled choir because voice gone. Lift home 3.30, or walk after clubs. S.* I thought perhaps I might earn some points by being sympathetic, so I skipped aerobics and went home with Shirley at half-past three.

That was how, at four o'clock, I came to be cycling

back from the pharmacy in High Street with a supply of cough syrup and throat lozenges in my bike basket. Freewheeling round the corner at the end of Markethill, I saw the war memorial and Goldie's Academy on the other side of the road. The strange thing was that I wasn't at all frightened. On the contrary, I felt perfectly at home.

Suddenly a loud electric bell shattered the quiet afternoon. The school doors opened and kids started spilling out onto the road. The boys were wearing grey trench coats and the younger ones had old-fashioned blue caps. The girls were dressed in blue tunics and grey blazers edged with yellow braid. I swerved to the edge of the pavement as they barged past me, swinging their leather satchels, music cases and hockey sticks. They were laughing and chattering, though I don't actually recall voices now.

As the crowd thinned out, I saw three familiar figures saunter through the main door and stop on the steps to talk. Ginger was one, but I'd seen enough of her. I was much more interested in the other two. Slowly I cycled along the gutter, peering at them between the railings. I thought the boy was quite handsome in a gangly way; he had clear skin, alert blue eyes and short, wheat-coloured hair. It was when his girlfriend turned towards me that I almost fell off my bike.

I know it sounds weird, but the dark girl was my sister Shirley. I don't mean the sad woman in Goldie Court, with her tired eyes and grey threads appearing in her black hair. The girl on the steps of Goldie's Academy was lithe and beautiful, Shirley as she must have been at

apartment on the next two Saturday afternoons. Shirley didn't come out of the study and each time, after we'd had a coffee, Zak asked if I'd like to go out.

Even these expeditions were disappointing, however. Zak didn't kiss me or even hold my hand. He didn't take me back to his den, or to Cavelli's. Instead we went to Two Wheels, a motorcycle showroom in Kennet Street, to get more brochures, and then to a music store in Mill Riggs. I hung around looking at pop CDs I couldn't afford, while Zak bought boxed sets of music by Schoenberg and Stockhausen.

"Maybe Miss Fairlie would like to borrow these," he said, as if sucking up to Shirley was likely to impress me.

Both times he left me on the pavement, because he had to meet a guy down town at half-past three. Not a lot to show for the time I'd spent styling my hair, choosing clothes and trying out different shades of eyeshadow. Still, I didn't entirely lose heart. If Zak wasn't interested in me, I reasoned, why was he bothering to see me at all?

On 19 January, Shirley and I received a letter from Grandma. It was unexpected, because she rarely wrote to us. We'd spoken to her regularly on the telephone since New Year, and she'd sent me a card of congratulation and a five-pound note to reward me for my good report. But she hadn't mentioned coming to visit us again, and Shirley had made her bad cold an excuse for not going to Glasgow. Her hands were sore, and I suspected that she didn't want Grandma to see her.

The mail came after we'd left for school in the morning, so we didn't find the letter until we got home. Shirley sat down on the sofa, put on her specs and opened it. I read it over her shoulder.

Glasgow: 18 January

   My dear Girls,

   I am sorry that I haven't seen you since November, especially as I shall not now see you for several weeks. My sister Alice has invited me to go and stay with her in Canada (all expenses paid) and I have decided to go. I enjoyed my fortnight with Mary at Dunoon, but generally I've spent too much time this winter sitting in the dark, brooding about the past. A change of scene and Alice's cheerful company will do me good, I think. I leave Glasgow on the morning of 25 January – not the day I would have chosen, but that was when a flight was available. I return on 10 March. I shall miss you, but I shall send you postcards. You have Alice's telephone number if you need to contact me.

   Take care of each other.

   With much love from your

   Grandma.

   P.S. Shirley, I think you need a tonic to get rid of your cold and improve your appetite. Go to the doctor, there's a good girl.

I watched Shirley's scarred hands folding up the letter and putting it back in the envelope.

"I'm sure it's a good idea," she said. "She needs a break and if anyone can comfort her, Alice can. They're best friends and Alice loves spoiling Grandma."

I only knew Great-aunt Alice, who was my godmother, as a generous sender of presents and information about Canada.

"Have you ever met Alice?" I asked Shirley curiously.

"Yes, once. She came to stay when you were a baby," Shirley replied. "A little round twinkly person, not a bit like Grandma."

"How much younger?"

"About five years. She must have been a bright girl, coming from such a poor family to become an architect."

"Married?" I asked.

Shirley shook her head.

"No. Divorced, I think. We must remember to phone Grandma before she leaves," she said.

Which we did, several times. But either Grandma was out or she wasn't answering the phone.

14

Burns Night

Three days later, in dark and wintry weather, Shirley found some snowdrops and put them in my room. When I saw them, I wanted to cry. There was no ill will between Shirley and me. Since our spectacular quarrel she'd been perfectly pleasant, and I'd never have said the hurtful things to her that I used to say. But the flame of intimacy that had flickered between us at Christmas had died, and the pain was worse than if it had never been kindled.

My friendship with Zak was the only barrier between us, but it was a huge one. I didn't enjoy making Shirley anxious. I knew that she spent every break in classes worrying about where I was and with whom, and that I was making her Saturday afternoons hell. Sometimes I longed to tell her, truthfully, that she really had nothing to worry about, but pride prevented me. Zak had apologised. He seemed to be doing all he could to make up for his bad behaviour. Shirley was in the wrong.

In spite of everything, the little blue jug of snowdrops meant a lot to me. When I'd changed my shoes, I went to

Shirley's study. I found her sitting at her desk, her reading lamp poised over the exam script she was marking. She was surrounded by the books, files and sheaves of paper that nowadays were her whole life.

"Thank you for the snowdrops," I said. "They're lovely."

"Mum's favourite flowers," Shirley replied. She went on totting up marks on the paper in front of her but, as I was turning away, she put down her pen. "Alice, sit down a minute. I want to ask you something."

I knew it wasn't about Zak, because she would never quiz me. I moved a pile of exercise books from the spare chair and sat down. Shirley took off her glasses and rubbed her eyes.

"I have a problem," she said. "On Thursday the senior school is having a Burns Night. Since I didn't go to any of the Christmas events, I think I ought to turn up. But I can't leave you alone here, the way things are."

"Oh, God, Shirley," I said, suddenly upset. "This is terrible. You have no social life."

Shirley flicked her fingers dismissively.

"I'm not in the mood for social life," she said. "But work's different, so I wondered if you'd like to come to the Burns Night with me. I think you'd enjoy it. Besides, it might be good to have something to do – on that date especially."

"That date" was the first anniversary of the plane crash that had killed our parents, the date when Grandma would have preferred not to fly the Atlantic. We'd agreed that we'd try to treat it as just another day but, as it approached, depression hung over us like a black cloud.

"I'd like to come," I said, "only I won't know anyone, will I?"

"I'd thought of that," Shirley replied. "I have a nice sixth-year tutorial group who say they'll be glad to look after you."

"Then yes, thanks," I said gratefully. "What shall I wear?"

Shirley considered this.

"How about your grey suede skirt," she suggested, "and your pink shirt from Jigsaw? You can borrow my grey tights if your horrible cat hasn't torn them to shreds. And –" her full lips curved in a ghost of her old smile "– perhaps your black patent shoes rather than your Timberland boots, Alice."

I looked round the study for something to throw at her, but couldn't see anything that wouldn't damage her seriously.

I had never been to a Burns Night before, but I knew the form. Every year on 25 January there were hundreds of these parties, held to celebrate the birthday of Robert Burns, Scotland's best-known poet. The main dish was haggis, a minced meat and oatmeal pudding much eaten in Scotland long ago. People made speeches and there was a concert of Burns' poems and songs. When I ran into Zak in school and told him I was going, he was enthusiastic.

"That's cool," he said. "You'll hear – but no. I think I'll keep it for a surprise."

"Please tell," I begged, but he wouldn't.

With a wink and a provoking grin, he went off to his next class.

On Thursday evening I felt quite shy as I arrived in the school hall with Shirley. The place was full of teachers and seniors who were at least two years older than me. Shirley, looking mega stylish in a short black dress and cerise embroidered shawl, quickly introduced me to the seniors who were going to look after me.

"Rab, Mhairi, Helen," she said. "This is Alice."

As the three seniors took me away to meet their mates, I saw Mr Gray from the Science department moving in on Shirley.

"Mr Gray fancies Miss Fairlie," Mhairi told me mischievously.

"Don't we all?" grinned Rab.

At one end of the dining-room there was a long table, spread with a white cloth. Other tables, laid for one teacher and five pupils, were set at right angles to it. I wasn't thrilled to see that the teacher at my table was Mr Gibbons, also known as "Wee Ferdy". He didn't teach me, but everybody said he was the stupidest prat on the planet. Still, I supposed it might have been worse. I might have got old Falc or Granny Clark.

Old Falc and Granny Clark, it turned out, were too important to sit with me. When the "top table" filed in, I saw the headmaster Mr Croy and his wife, Mr Falconer, the head boy and head girl, Granny Clark and, to my surprise, Zak Petersen.

All the rest were in conventional clothes, but Zak was wearing a red kilt and furry sporran. He had on a black velvet jacket with silver buttons and lace ruffles at his wrists and throat. I thought he looked stunning, and was a bit peeved by the incredulous sniggers of the boys at my table. As he sat down, Zak caught my eye, winked and wiggled his fingers. I wiggled mine back.

I looked furtively to see whether Shirley, who was at the next table, had noticed, but she was too busy wowing the kids sitting with her. Mr Falconer must have noticed, though. Leaning forward in his chair, he was gazing at Zak with an expression of almost idiotic admiration in his faded eyes. Only when a piper appeared, leading in a girl in a tartan frock and frilly cap, did he tear his gaze away.

"That's supposed to be Poosie Nancy," Rab informed me, "and the grey thing like a fat rat she's carrying is your supper. She was the barmaid at the pub where Burns went to get plastered," he added, "according to your sister."

"Only she put it more politely," said Helen repressively.

Fortunately, haggis tastes better than it looks. As we tucked in, Wee Ferdy Gibbons started a stupid argument with the boys about whether Robert Burns would have supported Celtic or Glasgow Rangers F.C. I listened to the girls, who were talking about Shirley.

"God, would you look at that shawl," sighed Helen, a large, rosy girl with long fair hair. "And these ear-rings! She makes me despair."

"Yeah, she's lovely," agreed Mhairi, who was short and

brown, like me. "You're lucky to have such a nice big sister, Alice."

"Yes, I know," I said.

I was fascinated to see a Shirley unknown to me, a teacher with her kids. She was completely absorbed, leaning on her elbow as she listened to their stories, laughing and encouraging them, making them feel good. Only I knew what it was costing her.

"Alice," said Helen, "don't mind me asking this. What's wrong with Miss Fairlie's hands?"

"Stress," I said.

"Ach, the poor wee lamb," said Mhairi sympathetically. "I hope it's not our fault."

"No, she loves you to bits," I assured her. "It started when our mum and dad died. It comes and goes."

Their concern and affection for Shirley touched me although, as much of her stress was down to me, it also made me ashamed.

By the time the tables were cleared and glasses of juice passed round for us to drink toasts, the heat in the dining-room was terrific. Condensation was running down the windows, and jackets and shawls were being shrugged off. As Mr Falconer made a boring speech about what Robert Burns would have thought of Millkennet High, I almost fell asleep. Alerted by the scraping of chairs as people rose to drink to Burns' "Immortal Memory", I forced my eyes open and caught a glimpse of Shirley.

It was obvious that she was wilting too. Her carefully applied make-up was fading in the heat and she was panda-eyed with exhaustion. When she caught my eye, however, she raised her eyebrows and smiled. I grinned back, looked at my watch and wished fervently that it was time for bed.

I can barely remember what came next. I have a confused memory of more speeches, including one from Granny Clark that drew huge laughs and foot-stamping applause. I think poems were recited and the school ceilidh band played. I know that Helen put her arm round me to stop me falling off the chair. At last I was jerked awake by Mr Croy's booming voice.

"Finally, ladies and gentlemen, it gives me pleasure to introduce Zak Petersen, who will close our Burns Night with a song."

So this was the surprise Zak had promised me! Wide awake now, I eagerly watched him stride to the piano. My pleasure was intense – but very brief. The notes of the introduction alerted me. My throat tightened and apprehension crept like furry caterpillars over my skin.

> *"Ae fond kiss, and then we sever!*
> *Ae fareweel, alas, for ever!*
> *Deep in heart-wrung tears I'll pledge thee,*
> *Warring sighs and groans I'll wage thee."*

It wasn't only the same song that Shirley and I had heard over and over again in Goldie Court. *It was the same voice*. Wide-eyed, I looked at Shirley, but she wasn't looking at me. With her hands clenched to stop them trembling, she was staring at Zak with the spellbound intensity of a rabbit face to face with a snake.

> *"Had we never loved sae kindly,*
> *Had we never loved sae blindly,*
> *Never met – or never parted,*
> *We had ne'er been broken-hearted."*

As the searing words of doomed love rang through the room, I turned my eyes away from my sister's suffering. To my horror, I saw another haunted face. Mr Falconer wasn't looking at Zak now. It took me a moment to realise that he was staring at Shirley. I have never seen such a sad, lonely, remorseful look on a human face.

> *"Fare thee weel, thou first and fairest!*
> *Fare thee weel, thou best and dearest!*
> *Thine be every joy and treasure,*
> *Peace, enjoyment, love and pleasure!"*

There was a scatter of applause, but also a swell of hissing and growling that would have bothered me had I been able to take it in. At least Mr Falconer didn't hear it. As Zak stood smiling ironically, taking exaggerated bows, his grandfather rose from the table. Mopping his face with a handkerchief, he tottered away towards the door.

When I'd put on my coat and said goodbye to Mhairi and Helen, I waited for Shirley in the vestibule. She came out of the staff-room with her friends, but left them abruptly when she saw me. I put my hand into hers and we walked out together into the frostbound, star-embroidered night.

Sometimes you don't talk because you can't. As we waited in the car for the windscreen to demist, I felt as if my tongue was welded to the roof of my mouth. I reckoned Shirley felt the same. As we drove the short distance home, the kids tumbling down Corngate waved to us cheerfully. I waved back and Shirley sounded the horn. Going upstairs to the apartment, she put a sheltering arm round my shoulders.

If I see the ghost tonight, I thought, I'm going to scream the place down. But there was no ghost, and the apartment was so quiet that later, when I was in bed, I could hear Shirley crying through the wall.

15

An Unpopular Appointment

Why didn't I go into Shirley's bedroom that night and try to comfort her? Not because I didn't care, but because I didn't know how. As I writhed in the dark, sweating and biting my nails, I understood for the first time how that cruel song of broken promise had been hurting my sister. I had a piercing memory of Mum fetching her own wedding dress and giving it to Shirley the day she got engaged to Toby Halliday. I remembered Shirley putting the dress on and dancing hand in hand with me around the room.

Now I realised something unbearable. Shirley had loved Toby so much that, in a way, losing him had been worse than death. The years we'd spent with Mum and Dad would always be ours, a happy, unstained memory. But Shirley knew that somewhere Toby was alive, married to another woman, probably having children with her. This was grown-up love, light-years removed from the desire to walk out with a cool guy and be seen with him at Cavelli's. It was no wonder Shirley looked so unhappy. She was being tortured by a song.

As for the way Zak's voice had echoed – no, had *been* – the voice we heard in Goldie Court, that was weird beyond understanding, as was the grief on Mr Falconer's face when he looked at Shirley. Imprisoned in a damp tangle of bedclothes, I heard the parish church clock strike every hour between twelve and four. Not until the strangled sobbing next door had finally died away did I fall asleep.

When I stumbled into the kitchen at ten to eight, Shirley was drinking black coffee at the table. She looked the way I felt – totally wrecked. I thought we both needed a morning in bed, but Shirley didn't make concessions to herself and the time when I would have spent a day alone in the apartment was long past. As I came out of my bedroom with my book bag, Shirley gave me a quick, apologetic smile.

"I'm sorry about last night," she said. "I'm afraid I kept you awake. I'm all right now, but – oh, Alice! If only it were some other song."

"What I hate," I burst out angrily, "is seeing what's happening to you and not knowing why."

Shirley picked up her car keys.

"Never mind, poppet. Easter's early this year," she said.

When I got out of the car, I was aching with lack of sleep. The day stretched before me, so wearisome that I wished I'd had the courage to stay in my bed. If I had, however, I'd have missed what, in the humdrum world of school, was an event – and I wouldn't have heard a strange but important story.

On Friday morning, Millkennet High School had an

Assembly before classes began. Mr Croy stood at a reading desk, with the teachers trying not to yawn behind him on the platform. We sang a hymn, if you could call it singing when nobody knew either the words or the tune. Mr Croy gabbled a prayer, desperate to get on to his weekly lecture about the sinfulness of spray-painting football slogans and throwing sweetie papers in the flower beds. We all sat like zombies, our eyes glazed with boredom. The chance of anything but the fire-alarm rousing us was remote. But, once in a blue moon . . .

"As many of you know," said Mr Croy, "Mr Hugh Falconer, our principal teacher of English, is retiring at Easter. During the past week, interviews have been held to find a worthy successor. I am pleased to announce that Mr Fergus Gibbons has been appointed to succeed Mr Falconer next term."

He wiggled his moustache, waiting for the polite if limp-handed applause that usually greeted this kind of announcement. Who cared, after all? But Wee Ferdy Gibbons was a school joke. He looked like a monkey in trendy specs. He made spelling mistakes on the blackboard and the reek of his aftershave would have felled an elephant. The notion of him being principal teacher of a paper bag was right off the wall.

There was a gasp, not to say a snigger, of disbelief, then someone at the back of the hall started slow hand-clapping. In seconds we had all joined in. The teachers shuffled and looked shifty, while Mr Croy's cheeks turned slowly blue. He roared for silence, but no one paid any attention. To the contemptuous and unstoppable rhythm, he was forced to lead his po-faced staff out of the hall. Then we all laughed.

"At Goldie's Academy fifty years ago," said Shirley severely, "the headmaster would have belted the lot of you."

It was seven o'clock and Shirley and I were already in our dressing-gowns. Sitting at the kitchen table, we were sharing a salad before having a very early night.

"He could hardly have belted five hundred of us," I pointed out, giggling. "Did Mr Croy want to belt us?"

As Shirley had descended from the platform in the morning, she had looked as snooty and offended as any of her colleagues. Now she couldn't help laughing.

"I wouldn't go that far, but he wasn't best pleased," she grinned. "Nor was the new principal teacher. His wee face was all a-tremble."

I dipped a slice of cucumber in mayonnaise and ate it. Then I took a risk.

"The kids all say it should've been you," I said.

Shirley raised her black eyebrows.

"Do they, now?" she said. "Then you can do something for me on Monday. Start whispering that I didn't apply for the job."

I took another risk.

"Why not?" I asked.

Shirley rested her chin on her hand. I knew she was wondering whether to break her rule of not discussing teachers' business with me. I think that night she just needed to talk, and she didn't have anyone else.

"Alice," she warned, "this is private. Just you and me, OK?"

"OK," I agreed.

"Well," said Shirley, "it's all a bit strange. I'd really have liked the job, but even before it was advertised, Mr Falconer told me I'd be wasting my time if I applied. He said he wouldn't support me or give me a reference."

I could feel my jaw almost hitting the table.

"But – but why?" I stammered.

Shirley sighed.

"He wouldn't say," she replied. "I can't deny I was hurt. I have a good degree and as much experience as any of the people they interviewed – who must've been pretty crummy if Ferdy was the pick of the bunch. It isn't as if Mr Falconer can complain about my commitment. He gave up on the job when his wife died, and I'm the one who covers for him. Since September I've done two-thirds of his teaching and almost all his paperwork."

"What?" I gasped, understanding suddenly why Shirley lived like a mole in her study, looked half-dead and couldn't find time to move house. "But that's criminal. Why don't the other teachers help you?"

Shirley shrugged feebly.

"They have children, they have houses to decorate, they have old grannies in hospital," she said. "Meaning, it's not their job."

"So why do you –?"

"For the kids, Alice," said Shirley wearily. "In a community like this, decent schooling's their only hope of a better life than their parents have had. I had a very

95

privileged education, and now I want to give something back."

"I wish you taught me," I blurted out.

Shirley smiled indulgently.

"I'd like to teach you," she said, "but what happened to embarrassment?"

I felt myself going pink.

"That was before I found out you were a star," I explained. "You're a smash hit with the sixth-years and Zak says it would be cool to be related to Miss Fairlie."

"Not for Miss Fairlie," snapped Shirley.

Aware that I was on a dangerous path, I reversed speedily.

"I'd like to kill that old Falc," I growled.

Shirley didn't respond. She sat frowning and winding a strand of hair round her finger.

"I suppose I shouldn't have been surprised," she said eventually. "Although he's so dependent on my help, he's never liked me."

"Don't be silly!"

"No, it's true. When we're talking, he won't even look at me. He calls the others in the department by their forenames, but he calls me 'Miss Fairlie'. When Mum and Dad died, the people at Millkennet High were perfect to me. I was hugged by teachers and kids I hardly knew. Mr Falconer put a note in my pigeon-hole. It said, 'Mr and Mrs Hugh Falconer express condolences to Miss Fairlie on the loss of her parents.' I wouldn't have gone back this year if I hadn't known he was retiring, or perhaps –" she laughed ruefully "– if I had known that come the summer term I'd be working for Ferdy Gibbons."

"Do you want to leave?" I asked, but Shirley refused to be drawn.

"After Easter," she promised, "when you and I are living in some peaceful place, we'll decide together what our future is to be."

I watched her get up and begin to clear the table.

"Shirley," I said, "may I ask you something?"

"If you must."

"Do you think it's Zak's voice we hear singing here?"

Shirley looked startled.

"Oh no. It couldn't be," she said.

"Then do you think –"

Shirley came behind me and gently cupped her hand over my mouth.

"Sweetheart," she said, "I'm too tired to think. Let's go to bed."

16

The Lovers' Tree

As it happened, the question Shirley was too tired to think about was answered by someone else the very next day.

At ten to two on Saturday afternoon, Grandma phoned from Canada. Her voice came on the answering machine, which Shirley had switched on while we were hoovering. She was roaring, presumably because Toronto was such a long way from Millkennet.

"Shirley! It's your grandma. I know you're there. *Shirley!* Pick up the phone this minute. This is costing money."

Gnashing her teeth, rolling her eyes and reducing me to a wild fit of giggles, Shirley obeyed orders. I listened with my face buried in a cushion.

"Grandma! How lovely to hear your voice. Did you have a good flight? . . . Oh, you were flying first class! All right for some . . . Niagara Falls? Well, you'll enjoy that . . . What d'you mean, have I been to the doctor? My cold's better. I'm fine, honestly . . . Alice? No, she can't talk. Sorry, I can't see her face anywhere . . ."

At this point the buzzer was pressed downstairs and I

ran to let Zak in. Shirley was putting the phone down as I opened the apartment door.

"Wow! Miss Fairlie!" cried Zak delightedly, ignoring me completely as he stepped into the hall.

Shirley burst out laughing. Perhaps she'd decided that playing the wicked witch in my love life was counter-productive. Perhaps she was in a mellow mood because she'd had a decent night's sleep. Instead of bolting into her study, she went back into the sitting-room and sat down on the sofa. Zak pranced after her.

"Well hey, Miss Fairlie," he gushed, dropping into an armchair, "you were looking cool on Thursday night. Great frock. Prada?"

"Jasper Conran, actually," said Shirley. Unable to repress a grin, she added, "Where did you get yours? Not your usual cool chic, if you don't mind my saying so."

Zak guffawed.

"God! I didn't buy it," he said. "Catch me spending money on tat like that. It belonged to my granddad when he was at school in the 1950s. He was the lead singer with the Goldie's Academy ceilidh band. The sporran had moths in it, and I've had the kilt hanging up in the garage since Christmas, trying to get rid of the cheesy smell."

"That explains it," murmured Shirley, a remark which no doubt meant something different to Zak from what it meant to me. "You sang – so beautifully. How's your bassoon coming along?"

Zak was boasting in his cool, ironic manner when she got up suddenly and, without a word, wandered off to the study. Zak's eyes widened in amazement.

"Am I so boring?" he asked.

"No, it's her. Teachers, you know – it gets to them," I replied disloyally.

"Yeah, I've noticed," laughed Zak. "Well, mush mush, Alice!" he added, jumping from his chair. "I've something to show you, but I don't have all day."

This is what it would be like having a big brother, I thought impatiently, as I went to put on my fleece. Nothing but cheek and ordering you about as if you were a husky. I felt curious, just the same.

Once we were out in the pallid afternoon, Zak made straight for a gate between Goldie Court and the railway bridge, which led into the public park. Although our sitting-room overlooked trees at the top of the park, I'd never set foot in it before. It was an intimidatingly vast green space, sadly underused and usually deserted. Even the children's swings and roundabouts were rusty and forlorn. Just inside the gate, Zak pointed to a neglected sandstone wall.

"This was the boundary wall of Goldie's Academy," he told me. "My grandparents were both pupils there. Here's the gate they used to get from the school grounds into the park."

"Imagine," I murmured. It went through my mind that I knew a fat lot more about Goldie's Academy than Zak ever would, but I looked politely at the paltry traces of that once proud school. At the corner of the wall, where the ground dipped sharply towards a waterlogged football pitch, Zak paused.

"There was a putting green over there," he said, waving his hand like a tour guide. "Below the fountain was a bandstand – you can still see an outline on the grass. The swings were for the little kids, and this path was called the Sixth-Form Walk." He began to run along a neglected asphalt footpath, winding among the trees whose branches laced our sitting-room window. I trotted like a spaniel at his heels. The path ended where a huge sycamore cast a dark net on the winter sky. "The Lovers' Tree," said Zak dramatically, then burst into hoots of laughter.

The name was easy to understand. The smooth grey trunk was scarred with names and initials: *Liam loves Betty*: *P Rowe & A McKinnon*: *SL XXXX PB*. Outstanding, because it was so deeply carved, was a large heart, like on a Valentine card. An arrow pierced it between two sets of initials, *HF* and *JF*. "Your grandparents?" I suggested.

Zak spluttered.

"No! Hugh Falconer and Another – my granddad's secret love. He won't tell anyone who it was and my gran used to go ballistic if it was even mentioned. Can you imagine old Falc with a secret love?"

It went through my mind that if Zak had known how deeply I hated his grandfather, he wouldn't have been so chirpy.

"I suppose it's quite sweet," I said insincerely.

Perhaps the word irritated Zak, because his smooth face suddenly hardened.

"They were so bloody naive, that generation," he said disparagingly. "They thought making love was giving each other a goodnight kiss after the Saturday dance. They just can't understand that the world's moved on."

I didn't know how to reply. I was sucking my teeth and

feeling uncomfortable when I had an unexpected but familiar sensation. An icy draught billowed through the trees, chilling my skin and ruffling the limp winter grass.

Whirling round, I saw the ghost standing only a few metres away. Except for the first time, when I'd seen her in the memorial garden, I'd never seen her out of doors. Her body seemed smokier and more brittle, but her chalky face and wild red hair were as vivid as ever. For once, she was showing no interest in me. With an expression of shocking intensity in her eyes, she was staring at Zak. Silent tears were pouring down her cheeks and her pinched mouth trembled piteously.

It amazed me that anyone could be the subject of such consuming attention and not notice. I gasped when Zak turned his back on the Lovers' Tree and strode away across the grass. He passed the ghost nonchalantly, almost brushing her outstretched hand. It was she who shrank away from him, fading among the trees like an unheard cry. When I caught up with him, Zak was already at the gate.

"Zak," I said breathlessly, "do you believe in ghosts?"

His lip-curling scorn reminded me sharply of our first encounter.

"Oh, get real," he barked, walking away from me into the bitter afternoon.

Feeling choked and disappointed, I went dismally indoors. As I let myself into the apartment, however, I heard something so unusual that it drove Zak and his moods right out of my mind. In the sitting-room, Shirley was swearing furiously. Cautiously I peeped round the door.

To my horror, I saw that our beautiful room had been trashed. CDs and cushions were strewn everywhere. A vase of white tulips had been overturned, the curtains were hanging half off their poles and the floor was covered with shards of glass. Half grown narcissi were scattered on the pale carpet and Shirley was on her knees, sweeping up bulb fibre and fragments of a red and gold china bowl.

"Burglars!" I screamed. "Shirley, are you all right?"

Shirley stopped cursing and scrambled to her feet.

"I'm fine, but that cat of yours needs a psychiatrist," she said.

"Oh, no," I moaned. "What happened?"

Shirley wiped her hands absent-mindedly on her white linen shirt.

"About ten minutes ago," she told me, "I came in here to fetch a book. The cat was sitting quietly on the windowsill, looking out into the park. Suddenly he went berserk – yowling and spitting and throwing himself around the room – as you see."

I was so appalled, I began to cry.

"Oh, Shirley," I wailed. "Your lovely room, and Mum's Japanese bowl! I'm so sorry."

Shirley tutted and offered me a paper handkerchief.

"There, there," she said kindly. "Don't cry. They're only things. But I do wonder if that poor beast needs treatment."

"Where is he now?" I sobbed.

"In my bed, I expect," replied Shirley with grim humour.

17

Men of Millkennet

Clearing up the sitting-room took ages. Shirley had to borrow a ladder from the Huntlys next door so that we could rehang the curtains, but it was sweeping up glass and cleaning marks off the carpet that took most time. When at last we'd finished, everything was tidy, though the shelves were noticeably barer than before.

"Less to pack when we move," said Shirley philosophically.

Sooty wasn't in Shirley's bed – he wasn't that stupid. Aware that he was in her bad books, he had stalked off to his basket in the kitchen. When I looked in, he was lying with his face turned huffily to the wall.

Of course, I knew why Sooty had wrecked the sitting-room. He'd behaved in exactly the same way the day he'd seen the ghost from the kitchen window. It seemed a shame that I couldn't defend him to Shirley but, since I was still determined to hide the whole truth about my haunting, Sooty would have to live with being misunderstood.

At six o'clock I made coffee and salad sandwiches. Shirley, now well behind with Mr Falconer's paperwork, took hers into the study. I ate mine in the kitchen, enjoying the quiet that was still holding, then went to my room to revise some Geography. I was in the running for a prize for my project on Canada, so I wanted to do well in the test we were having on Monday. Unfortunately, nothing interested me less just then than the land distribution and population of Canada. After five minutes, I abandoned my desk and flopped down on my bed. Closing my eyes, I visualised the heart on the Lovers' Tree. With a desperation I couldn't understand, I longed to know whose initials Mr Falconer had carved along with his own.

This wasn't just idle curiosity. In one way, I couldn't have cared less about the love life of a miserable old teacher who'd been bewilderingly cruel to my sister. But it wasn't that simple. However much I despised him, Mr Falconer had invaded our lives. He'd become more important than his manky appearance and mean spirit deserved.

What Zak had told us confirmed what Shirley had been too tired to contemplate, that Mr Falconer had been the boy we heard singing – a ghost in Goldie Court, a living person outside. But why should we hear him? What was the significance of that old Scots love song, so meaningful yet hurtful to Shirley? It was hard to believe that the aching words had meant nothing to the schoolboy who sang them so tenderly. They had certainly upset his older self on Thursday night.

So who had been in his mind? Not Shirley Fairlie, who would be unborn for another twenty years. Was it the person whose initials he had carved on the Lovers' Tree? If so, I supposed that the red-haired ghost was a candidate. Her distress at Zak's scoffing laughter would be understandable if the initials were hers. On the other hand, since Mr Falconer was only sixty-four, it was perfectly possible that his secret love was still alive.

It's difficult to know just how the wires of your mind connect, flashing an answer to a question you thought was unfathomable. Ever since the night when I'd discovered that Shirley was also haunted, I'd asked myself something over and over again. Why had "something unnatural" been unleashed in Goldie Court that concerned only us two? Until now, I'd failed to see any connection between us and young people who'd lived in Millkennet fifty years ago. But, of course, there was a connection. It was Grandma.

What had put me off the track was Shirley's insistence that Grandma couldn't have gone to Goldie's Academy. I didn't dispute this; I just didn't think it was important. What was important was that something so terrible had happened to Grandma in Millkennet that she wouldn't even come to lunch with her own granddaughters.

Suppose for a moment that Grandma had known Hugh Falconer, been his girlfriend even, when she lived in Millkennet long ago. You didn't have to go to the same school or even belong to the same social group for that – it was just more likely that your relationship would come to grief. Was it possible that Grandma wouldn't come back to Millkennet for the same reason that Shirley wouldn't go back to Cambridge? Could the initials on the tree be hers?

I may not have the biggest brainbox in our family, but I'm not stupid either. I know the difference between speculation and proof. Grandma's married name was Jean Mercer. Even if her maiden name, which I didn't know, began with F, it wouldn't prove a thing. All the same, I terribly wanted to find out.

Which I could have done, I suppose, by going across the hall and asking Shirley. But it was a peculiar question to ask without giving a reason and I really didn't fancy trying to explain. My clever sister had a genius for demolishing even well-constructed arguments, and mine certainly wasn't that. Besides, for all the deep love between them, Shirley had a closed mind about Grandma.

Because Grandma had been a nursemaid in her youth, didn't talk about books and thought Schoenberg's music was a big noise, Shirley reckoned she was just an uncultured old wifie. I wanted to avoid a basilisk stare of incredulity if I suggested that Grandma might once have had a love affair with an educated young man. Even if Grandma's name had been Fulton or Forsyth, it would be dismissed by Shirley as sheer coincidence.

It would make sense, I decided, to do a bit of private research first, and something Shirley had once said gave me an idea where I might begin.

On Sunday afternoon, something happened that should have made the whole day bright. At half past two, when Shirley was working and I was getting ready to go out alone, the entryphone buzzed. When I picked up the handset, a voice said, "Hi, Alice. It's Louise. Can I come in?"

I was absolutely delighted. Since I came to Millkennet, this was the first time a classmate had dropped in to see me at home. What's more, if I'd been able to choose, I'd have chosen Louise Carter. She had a perky face and twinkly eyes, and when she laughed you were amazed that such a big noise could erupt from such a tiny body. When I opened the door she bounced in, grinning under a grey furry hat. She was wearing a matching jacket and pink fluorescent boots.

"Fancy a coffee at Cavelli's?" she asked.

These were words I'd longed to hear, but I'd already made a plan for the afternoon. I thought quickly.

"I'd love to," I said. "Can you come somewhere with me first?"

"Yip. I've finished my homework so I've loads of time. Where d'you want to go?" asked Louise.

"The war memorial," I replied, sticking my purse in the pocket of my fleece.

Before I went out, I put my head round Shirley's door.

"My friend Louise is here," I said. "We're going to Cavelli's for a coffee."

If Shirley was pleased, she was careful not to show it.

"Good. Have a nice time," she said.

"If this isn't a stupid question," said Louise, as we headed down Corngate under the pink winter sun, "why are we going to the war memorial? Don't tell me somebody's dead."

"My great-grandfather," I grinned. "I'm doing a bit of family history and I want to check up on him."

"Right on," nodded Louise. "Let's jog to the memorial,

then we can have jam doughnuts with our coffee at Cavelli's."

I didn't ask whether she thought she had a weight problem, or was concerned about mine.

It was a strange experience seeing the memorial, not rising out of its ruff of shrubs, but hemmed in by buildings three times its height. It was less imposing, but certainly the same one. Now enclosed in a paved courtyard with a wrought-iron gate, the stone soldiers gazed out indifferently across the busy road. I'd never been close enough to the memorial to read what was carved on it but, as Louise opened the gate, I saw these words on the front of the plinth:

IN PROUD MEMORY
OF THE MEN OF MILLKENNET
WHO GAVE THEIR LIVES IN
THE GREAT WAR
1914 – 1918
WE WILL REMEMBER THEM

On the other three sides were long bronze plaques listing a tragic number of names, but giving no indication of where these young lives were lost.

"Which war did your ancestor die in?" asked Louise.

"Second."

"Then you'd better look over here."

Because there was no room for more names on the plinth, a flat sandstone wall had been built to hold additional plaques. It had dates too: 1939 – 1945. I suppose because there had been fewer casualties, there was space for more information. I felt a little flutter of excitement when I saw that the men of World War II had been listed under the countries where they'd died: Burma, Malaya, Germany, Italy, France.

"Can you see North Africa?" I asked eagerly.

"Yip, down here. Only three," Louise replied.

Even as I looked, I felt my excitement fading away.

Duncan Ross Capt Seaforth Highlanders
Forbes Stewart Lieut Seaforth Highlanders
Francis Cameron Pte Black Watch

It wasn't hard to guess which my great-grandfather had been – Private Francis Cameron of the Black Watch. My hunch about Grandma had been wrong, and my disappointment was so acute that I wanted to cry. Louise saw that I was upset and tried to console me.

"You should bring flowers some time," she suggested. "That would make you feel better. Now come on to Cavelli's."

As I jogged behind her along dingy Kennet Street, I reflected bitterly that my day couldn't get worse. Wrong yet again.

Cavelli's was about as hip as Millkennet could get. It was a long, mirror-lined café with smoked-glass tables and shiny black benches arranged back to back like in a railway carriage. The place wasn't busy, and Louise and I were soon tucked into a compartment with a caffè latte each and a plate with two jam doughnuts between us. I was doing my best to chat about the latest singles, and to remember whether Miss Fairlie's red shoes were Manolo Blahnik or Jimmy Choo, when I glimpsed, indirectly through a mirror, a couple sitting further down the café. To my horror, I recognised a heavy gold earring and a familiar crop of dyed blond hair.

Zak's companion was a girl I recognised from school, though I didn't know her name. She was about his age, with long, streaked hair and the kind of eye make-up that makes you look like a skull. Zak had his arm round her and, under my mortified gaze, he drew her towards him and kissed her. As they slid off the bench and went out into the street, their mouths were practically welded together.

"Was that Zak Petersen?" frowned Louise. "I can't stand that guy. He's just a waste of space."

18

A Nice, Caring Kind of Guy

In my experience, you can't worry seriously about more than one thing at a time. When I'd seen Francis Cameron's name on the war memorial and realised that my theory about Grandma was dead in the water, I'd felt completely gutted. By the time I got home, few things were further from my mind.

Sitting at my desk, trying yet again to cram some Geography into my head, I felt angry, stupid and deceived. OK, Zak Petersen had never made love to me, and I'd no one but myself to blame for my stupid dreams of romance. But he'd come to my place four Saturdays, had invited me out and seemed to enjoy my company. If he wasn't interested in me at all, why on earth had he bothered? As I slung my books into my bag for the morning, I was sure of only one thing. Whatever space Zak Petersen was wasting next Saturday, it wouldn't be mine.

My problem was finding an opportunity to warn him off. I couldn't ring him up, because Shirley was always in the apartment. There was no point in waiting in the vestibule, because he never came there any more. By Thursday, with the weekend rolling dangerously close, I was getting desperate. My only chance, I decided, was to waylay him as he came out of his last class in the afternoon. From the master timetable outside the school office, I discovered that this was French in room 18. Since I was in History in room 14, I wouldn't have to sprint too far.

For once, when the bell rang, I was at the front of the stampede for freedom. Charging up the corridor, I reached room 18 as the door opened and class 4B came barging out. Among them was Zak's skull-eyed girlfriend. Through the door I could see Zak packing his books into a posh leather holdall and giving cheek to the teacher. When he came swaggering into the corridor, I stepped forward and blocked his way.

"I want to talk to you," I said.

"Alice!" Zak grinned feebly and tried to dodge past me. "Not now," he pleaded. "I could murder for a coffee. Can't it wait till Saturday?"

"No," I said obstinately, staying in his way. "It's got to be now."

Zak hissed through his teeth. Just for an instant, a little frown like a snake's tongue creased his forehead. But then he glanced at his watch and said, "OK. Five minutes. Let's go in the cloakroom."

I thought it was as good a place as any to end a non-event. Among the broken pegs, greasy anoraks and sweaty trainers, I looked Zak right in the eye.

"It's over. Don't come round on Saturday," I said.

He had the kind of face that can assume an expression without moving a muscle. Now it was miffed surprise.

"Why on earth not?" he said. "I thought you liked our little outings."

It was the words "little outings" that got to me. I felt like a baby that had been taken out in its pram. Tears of humiliation rose in my eyes.

"It's over," I repeated tightly. "I saw you on Sunday –"

I was too choked to go on. Zak, who had perched himself on the edge of a washbasin, momentarily looked baffled. I saw his pale eyes widen as understanding dawned.

"I get it. You saw me with Lexie Reid, I suppose," he said. "Oh, get real, Alice! You never thought –? Did I ever give you that impression? You're a nice kid, but oh, God! What an idea!"

I had never felt so small.

"Then why?" I cried.

Zak hesitated, then shrugged ruefully.

"Oh, what the hell! If you must know, I was trying to get Brownie points from Miss Fairlie," he said.

I wondered if I was going mad.

"Brownie points?" I repeated stupidly. "I don't understand."

Zak spread his hands and gave a theatrical groan.

"What's to understand? When I realised I'd been – let's say, giving her the wrong message in the class, I wanted to get some extra points with her. You don't seem to have many mates, so I thought if I came round on Saturdays and took you out for an hour or so, she'd be pleased and think I was really a nice, caring kind of guy."

I still didn't latch on, but I can't blame myself. I was Alice in Cuckooland.

"Why should you care?" I asked sullenly.

To the end of my days, I'll never forget the self-satisfied smirk on his face, or his outrageous reply.

"Because ever since I went into her class, I've wanted to ask her out. She's brilliant – the only one in this dump besides myself with any style."

My jaw fell so far I almost had to catch it.

"For God's sake!" I spluttered. "She's a teacher. She's twenty-seven. You're only sixteen."

Zak pouted and gave another of his irritating shrugs.

"Seventeen next week, actually. Oh, come on, Alice! Be a good mate," he wheedled. "Put in a word for me. I'd be good for her and I like mature women."

I knew I was goggling, but his effrontery took my breath away. So this was why he'd come to the apartment, swanking around and sucking up to Shirley. What a stupid idiot he was – though not, let's face it, the stupidest idiot around. When I thought how Shirley would react, I could almost have laughed. Only when I remembered this creep at Cavelli's, wrapping himself round his girlfriend like a hungry snake, I felt more sick than amused.

"Well, here's news for you, Sunshine," I said contemptuously. "Even if you were a mature man, my sister wouldn't touch you with a bargepole. She doesn't just have style, you see. She has good taste."

I thought this was a fine speech and, as I stalked out of the cloakroom, I felt a surge of angry triumph. Only I didn't have long to enjoy it. Suddenly a heavy leather bag hurtled past my head, missing my nose by a centimetre. Smacking off the wall, it fell with a thud at my feet. Before I could step over it, Zak was out of the cloakroom. Slapping his palms on the wall, he imprisoned me between his long arms. I could feel his hot breath against my ear.

"Don't dare to speak to me like that, you stroppy little toerag," he spat. "I've let you get above yourself. Time for a change, eh?"

I was so scared I thought I was going to throw up on his leather jacket. But I was still angry enough for defiance.

"Shove off, Toadface," I said. "How can a weed like you hurt me?"

It was a stupid question, but I could never have imagined the cruelty of the reply. Zak gave one of his snakelike hisses, then dropped his voice to a gleeful whisper.

"Oh, I can hurt you," he said. "Just watch me. What was it you said that day when I let you give me lip in the vestibule? I'd made your sister's life hell. Well, here's news for *you*, Sunshine. I haven't even started."

My right hand was free, my nails were long and I had an overwhelming desire to spoil his face. I think I might have done it, if just then the fire door hadn't swung open. Through it came Rab Carter, dangling his football boots by their laces. Instantly Zak dropped his arms and picked up his bag.

"Hell starts period 2 on Monday," he said softly, smiling as he swung away from me along the corridor.

Rab watched him go with a look close to murderous.

"Is that freak bugging you, Alice?" he asked. Because I couldn't find words to tell him, I shook my head. "Well, there's a first," grinned Rab sceptically. "He sure is bugging everybody else." He was in the cloakroom doorway when he looked over his shoulder. "If you need a posse, I'm the sheriff," he said.

It was kind of Rab, and I was grateful. But as I stood shivering in the vestibule, waiting for Shirley to come out from choir practice, I didn't think there was a posse in the world that could help us now.

19

A Shadow Lifted

How long does it take a mouse to learn not to mess with a snake? I'd been warned over and over but wouldn't listen, and now I was to see my sister punished for my arrogance and stupidity. It was impossible to look at Shirley and believe that she could cope with another crisis. By this time next week she would be in a nursing home and I would be eating high tea in Aunt Ruth's stuffy little bungalow. Zak Petersen knew how to hurt me, all right.

I managed to get home without screaming, but there was no way I could last the evening without Shirley realising something was wrong. As we sat down to eat our chicken stir-fry, she peered anxiously at my moist red face.

"Alice, you've been crying," she said in surprise. "What's wrong, my love?"

Her kind tone was the last straw. To tell the truth just then would have choked me, but mercifully I had a credible lie to hand.

"I did badly in my Geography test," I snivelled, "and I don't think I'll get the prize."

Shirley's response was pure Grandma.

"Ach, pet, what does it matter? If you win a prize I'll be proud of you. If you don't, I'll love you just the same."

If I'd needed proof that, in spite of my wilfulness about Zak, my relationship with Shirley had changed for ever, I had it now. Six months ago she wouldn't have dared to say such a thing, for fear of being told what to do with her pride and affection. I felt a bigger skunk than ever.

I knew that I would have to tell Shirley everything before the snake struck on Monday but, when I'd pulled myself together enough to think, I decided to bide my time. This was only partly cowardice; I didn't see any point in shattering the fragile, unhaunted peace she was enjoying until I absolutely had to. Unusually for me, this was a good decision.

It's impossible to explain how a rumour runs round a school. You can be in class, with no opportunity to gossip. A guy comes in who's been to the loo, and in ten seconds the whisper's up and running. By three o'clock on Friday everybody knew that at one forty-five a police car had arrived at the front door. An hour later it had left with Zak Petersen and his mother in the back seat. No one but me seemed surprised.

"He's had it coming," said Louise dourly, as we put our gym kit in our lockers. "He's into drugs. My big brother Rab told me."

"Yeah, that's right," agreed Gillian. "No wonder everybody hates him. He's just scum."

119

Not long ago, these remarks would have hurt me badly, but no longer. I dare say I was heartless, but as I ran across the wet courtyard I felt nothing but wild relief. I had a key, so I opened the car and got in. I sat for ages, watching rain trickle down the windscreen like tears I couldn't shed.

Teachers came out of the school and hurried to their cars, grim-faced and hunched inside their waterproof coats. Shirley came out with Granny Clark. They stood for a moment sheltering under Shirley's pink umbrella. I saw them hug each other impulsively, then Shirley came running to the car. As she got in and shut the door, I said, "Is it true?"

Without looking at me, Shirley said, "Yes," and started the engine. She rarely talked when she was driving, but I knew she was in a frenzy. Her hand trembled between the steering-wheel and the gear lever, and her mouth looked as if it was closed over a scream. I was puzzled that she seemed to care so much about a boy of whom she had so little good to say. We were home in the sitting-room before I understood what was really tormenting her. Gripping my shoulders, Shirley looked straight down into my eyes.

"Alice," she said urgently, "tell me the truth. Do you know anything about this?"

Shocked and furious, I jerked away from her.

"No!" I exclaimed. "How could I?"

"You've been seeing Zak Petersen, haven't you?"

All the terror I'd caused her stared at me from her wide brown eyes. Filled with remorse, I put my hands on her thin arms.

"Listen," I said earnestly. "This is the truth, I swear it. I've only ever seen him on Saturday afternoons, and never for long because he always had to see a guy down town at half-past three. He never touched me and he never once mentioned drugs. Last Sunday when I was out with Louise, I saw him at Cavelli's with a girl – Lexie Reid, I think her name is. I realised I was making a fool of myself, so yesterday I told him to shove off. I was going to tell you at the weekend –"

I wouldn't have thought that Shirley's face could get any paler, but it did. Closing her eyes, she slid quietly through my hands onto the floor.

When Shirley came round, unnecessarily wet because I'd sloshed so much water on her face, I wanted her to go to bed, but she wouldn't.

"I'm all right now. I'll have a bath, then we must talk," she said.

So I cooked a pizza and beans for myself and made some toast for her. By seven o'clock we were curled up together on the sofa.

Shirley isn't a touchy-feely person. Even at the worst of times, she'd rarely cuddled me or held my hand. When people like that put an arm round your shoulders, it's usually because they need comforting themselves. I rubbed my head against her arm.

"I'm sorry I had to ask you that question," she said.

"I'm sorry I made you faint," I replied.

"Stupid of me," said Shirley. "I've just been so afraid for you, and this has been such a dreadful day."

"What has Zak done?" I asked.

Shirley tapped her fingernails restlessly on the arm of the sofa.

"If it's all true," she said, "he's part of a drugs ring. He's been spending school breaks selling narcotics in the Aiken Glen, and blackmailing his victims. He's been reported by other kids and the police have been watching him, but haven't moved because they needed to know who else was involved. If they'd nabbed Zak sooner, they'd have alerted his accomplices."

"The guy down town," I said.

"Yes. He was the barman at a nightclub where Zak hung out – illegally, since he's only sixteen. He certainly recruited Zak, but he's a small-time crook compared with some others. This morning the police raided several houses, including the Petersens'. Under Zak's study floor, they found hard drugs worth thousands of pounds."

I had a vivid memory of that desirable room, with its ostentatious display of gizmos no teenager could normally afford.

I said, "Why did he do it?" but I really knew the answer before Shirley spelt it out.

"Because he's greedy, because he's too conceited to think he'd ever be caught, because he has no sense of right and wrong," she said with barely concealed anger. "He isn't an addict, only a cold-blooded pusher. Someone happy to destroy the lives of sad, inadequate people for cashmere sweaters."

"Anyone we know?" I asked cautiously.

Shirley shook her head thankfully.

"The police are questioning two guys who hang around with him," she told me, "but no. His customers were edged his way by the guy at the nightclub. The police say this isn't a school problem. Teachers daren't be complacent, but today we're proud of our kids."

"Everybody hates Zak," I said. "I don't think anyone would buy a lollipop from him. Did you hear how they hissed him at the Burns Night? I used to think they were just jealous of his gear."

Shirley shook her head.

"No, it's far more than that," she replied. "He's a stuck-up prat and he can't leave other kids in peace. When he was younger, it was letting down their bike tyres and spilling water on their paintings. Now it's defacing their books and burning holes in their blazers."

"And kicking slush in their faces," I said, remembering the day I'd squared up to him in the vestibule.

"That sounds like him," agreed Shirley. "I've never been able to stand him, actually. There's something reptilian about him and I've always thought he could be really violent. However –" she touched my face with her forefinger "– if he hasn't taken advantage of you, that's something in his favour. And I must say, since you sorted him out, he's been no trouble to me."

I sensed her puzzlement, and knew that one day I would want to explain. But with the dark shadow of Zak's threat to her lifted, it didn't have to be now.

"What will happen to him?" I asked.

"That's for a court to decide," Shirley said. "He's young, but it's a very grave offence. The important thing is that he should get the help he needs. A big part of his problem has been his parents' refusal to admit there's anything wrong. Even today, when Mr Croy sent for her, his mother was all amazement. She said she assumed his father had been financing Zak. In one way, he's a spoilt brat, in another he's the most deprived kid I've ever met."

"He won't come back to Millkennet High, will he?" I asked.

I tried not to sound too anxious, but when Shirley said, "Definitely not," I couldn't restrain a deep sigh of relief.

"How has Mr Falconer taken this?" I inquired curiously.

Shirley shuddered.

"He's in shock," she said. "First he kept roaring that was impossible, then he started rocking to and fro and muttering to himself about a motorcycle."

"He was going to give Zak one for his birthday," I explained. "It cost nearly ten thousand pounds. And his father does send him money from Kuwait. You'd think he'd have enough."

"People like him never have enough," Shirley said.

At nine o'clock Shirley said she thought she'd get into bed, and I went to make tea. When I took it into her room, she patted the duvet and I curled up beside her again. I liked Shirley's room, which was airy and uncluttered; all it contained was her bed, an old chair from home, a pine chest of drawers and a small bookcase holding her childhood favourites – things like *The Lord of the Rings* and *Watership Down*. On a little shelf by the bed there was a photograph of Mum and Dad. They were at a barbecue in our back garden, wearing blue striped aprons and chefs' hats. They were holding up strings of sausages as if they were necklaces and grinning widely. When I looked at them I couldn't help grinning back.

After we'd drunk our tea, Shirley said, "Do you mind if I ask you something?"

"Of course not."

"Have you been very hurt by what's happened?"

All things considered, this wasn't an easy question to answer.

"I wasn't in love with him," I said eventually. "Not like you – anyway, not really in love. I thought at first that I might have liked him to kiss me, but what I really wanted was for other kids to see me holding hands with such a cool guy."

"Why?"

"So they'd think I was normal."

"Normal?" repeated Shirley uncertainly. "What do you mean, exactly?"

"I mean I'd like to have good mates and a boyfriend," I said painfully, "and be like other people again. Since Mum and Dad died, people don't treat me as if I was normal, Shirley."

I felt Shirley's hand gently twisting the hair at the nape of my neck. She was silent for a moment, then she said carefully, "I think you've got it the wrong way round, Alice. It isn't other people. It's something we feel about ourselves."

"Is it?"

"Yes. I have some good friends, but all this past year I've been avoiding them, partly because I've been afraid they were only inviting me out of pity and I've had enough of that already. But it was also because whenever I've caught myself enjoying something, I've felt I was betraying Mum and Dad."

This was exactly how I felt.

"On Saturday when Grandma rang up," I confessed, "I couldn't help laughing when you were talking to her. Afterwards I felt ashamed."

"I know. I'm sure it's a normal stage of grieving, but if it's passing, we mustn't cling to it. We'll have friends again when we're ready to be friends again, and I think that may even be now. Besides –" Shirley glanced at the photograph "– I don't think that crazy couple would want two daughters who couldn't laugh, do you?"

"No. Shirley, do you think Mum and Dad are ghosts now?"

I felt Shirley stiffen slightly, but she gave me an honest answer.

"If you'd asked me that a year ago, I'd have told you there was no such thing as a ghost. Now I can't do that. But I believe that happy people must be happy spirits, with no need to haunt the living. What's happening here is caused by some old, deep unhappiness. Perhaps we're sensitive to it because we've been unhappy too."

"I wonder if the ghosts will come back," I said.

Shirley left me to wonder.

"Hey, listen," she said. "How d'you fancy a day out

tomorrow? We'll have our hair cut and I'll get the grey bits tinted out of mine. Then we'll have a bite of lunch and see what's on at the cinema."

"Sounds cool," I said, "but do you feel well enough?"

Shirley rolled over and yawned.

"Now that I know you're safe," she said, "I feel better than I have for a long time."

I knew that her safety had been more at risk than mine.

"Shirley, I'm sorry I've been such a fool," I said. "Mum would be furious if she knew I'd turned your hair grey."

Shirley made a rude face.

"Don't flatter yourself," she retorted, hitching the duvet and tipping me onto the floor as if I was Sooty. "It's inherited. Don't tell me you hadn't noticed."

20

The Golden Treasury

I'd always hated February, a dead month of withered gardens, weepy skies and bitter grey afternoons. I'd been depressed by dirty pavements, spongy grass and soiled tatters of snow. This year the weather was the same, but I was different. Although I still had gloomy moments, this was my best time since I'd come to Millkennet.

At school I heard that I'd won the Geography prize after all. Louise started asking me to tea at her house on Tuesdays, and at the weekend she came to chill out at my place. I was invited to a couple of birthday parties, and a guy in my class, Andrew Parland, took me to McDonalds for Coke and a burger. He also sent me my only Valentine, scarcely a face-saver since Gorgeous Fairlie received thirty-four. We heard that Zak had been released on bail, and was staying with relatives in Edinburgh. The opinion at Millkennet High was that they should have locked him up and thrown away the key.

At Goldie Court, our apartment was so tranquil that it was hard to believe it was ever haunted at all. No doors banged, no plaintive voice sang, no rattling trains broke the peace of the night. I saw no ghost nor perplexing visions of Shirley as a schoolgirl, and I stopped dreaming about wells and stairs. Apart from his perverse, unrequited fondness for Shirley, Sooty reverted to being a sedate, well-adjusted cat.

Shirley too was benefiting from some peace and quiet. The rash on her hands faded and so did the dark shadows around her eyes. Her January marking complete, she was preparing her choir for the schools' music festival and having fun with the sixth-year play, Shakespeare's *Twelfth Night*. She also found time to talk to her solicitor about putting the apartment up for sale at Easter.

"Ferdy Gibbons's brother has a cottage in Dollar that we can rent for three months," she told me. "Who says Ferdy isn't a useful guy to know?"

Everything was going well, but there was one thing about Shirley that bothered me. In the early days in Millkennet, she'd been pretty laid-back when I went out, but now she was almost fretfully vigilant. When I went to Louise's house, I had to ring her and she came to fetch me, even though the Carters lived only two streets away. The day I went to McDonalds with Andrew Parland, she was at her bedroom window watching for me coming back. When, towards the end of the month, she began to have evening rehearsals of the play, she insisted on taking me with her. I got fed up sitting at the back of the hall, watching Rab tripping over his feet and Mhairi forgetting her lines for the umpteenth time. As my own nervousness receded, Shirley's protectiveness began to irk me, though I did my best to be patient. I reminded myself that she'd been through a lot, and that Easter was barely six weeks away.

Now that Shirley had less paperwork, I saw more of her. Usually after supper she went into her study while I did my homework, but later, after we'd had our showers, we messed about in the sitting-room, listening to music, reading magazines and painting our toenails. It was the part of the day I most enjoyed.

On the last evening in February, we'd been looking at the postcards Grandma had sent from Canada. She'd been to Niagara Falls, the Stratford Festival Theatre and to a lunch in Toronto where "wee Alice" was presented with an award for a school she'd designed. Her latest postcard was of the imposing National War Memorial in Ottawa, where she and Alice were staying with friends.

"That reminds me," said Shirley, turning the card over in her hands. "You were right that the war memorial here used to be across the road. Dorothy Clark says it was moved about ten years ago. There was a plan to make a traffic roundabout where Corngate meets Markethill, which would have cut into the memorial garden. Only as usual the council ran out of money and the roundabout never happened."

Nothing spooky about that, then.

"I went with Louise one Sunday," I remarked, "to look for Grandma's father's name."

"Did you find it?"

"Yes. He was a private in the Black Watch. His name was Francis Cameron."

Shirley, who was filing her fingernails, looked up in surprise.

"No, it wasn't," she said. "Francis was his surname."

I licked my lips, which suddenly felt dry.

"Are you sure?" I said cautiously. "There were only three men from here killed in North Africa. They were —" I racked my memory "— Duncan Ross, Forbes Stewart and Francis Cameron. The first two were officers, so I thought Francis Cameron must've been Grandma's father."

Shirley looked puzzled, then her face cleared.

"Oh, I see," she said. "They must have put the surnames first, like on a school register. It can be confusing, the Scottish custom of giving surnames as forenames."

Startled, I reversed the names in my head. Ross Duncan, Stewart Forbes, Cameron Francis — it was true that they all sounded just as likely the other way round.

"Did you know his forename was Cameron?" I inquired.

"No," replied Shirley, "but I know Grandma's name was Jean Francis. When she moved from Yoker to Dowanhill, she was getting rid of stuff and gave me some books. She'd written her name inside them."

"What kind of books?"

Shirley shrugged.

"I can't remember," she said. "They were old-fashioned and I never used them. I think I may still have one or two, though. Wait a minute."

Tense with excitement, I listened to her switching on the study light and exploring her bookshelves. Could it be that my idea about the Lovers' Tree was back on track? It seemed ages before Shirley returned, carrying three battered volumes which she tossed down on the sofa beside me. I looked at the spines and read: *Latin Grammar for Schools*,

Martin Chuzzlewit by Charles Dickens and *The Golden Treasury of English Poetry*. Opening the Latin grammar I saw, neatly written in faded ink, *Jean Francis, Form II, 1947-48.*

"Shirley," I said curiously, "if Grandma's as thick as you think she is, what on earth was she doing with books like these?"

Shirley didn't like this question at all.

"I've never said she was thick," she protested indignantly. "That's not a word I'd use about anyone. What I've said is that she's obviously uneducated – she has no interest in books or music or ideas. She doesn't have much respect for other people's education either."

Knowing this was a sore point, I didn't press it, but I wasn't going to give up.

"Why did she have a Latin grammar?" I persisted.

Shirley applied her nailfile impatiently.

"Everyone goes to school and she may have learned a little Latin," she said grudgingly.

I picked up *Martin Chuzzlewit*.

"She was in first year when she read this," I remarked. "Quite a fat read, Shirley. And think of all the ghastly old-fashioned books she gives me at Christmas. She *always* says, 'This was a favourite of mine when I was your age.'."

For the first time, I saw a flash of uncertainty in Shirley's eyes.

"That's true," she admitted. "I used to get them too – *The Vicar of Wakefield, Kenilworth*. God, they were boring."

"Well, then?"

Shirley put down her file and spread her hands helplessly.

"I don't know, Alice," she said. "I suppose it's unusual to know so little about your grandmother, but she's a very private woman. All I can tell you is that when I was little, she still worked for a family called Lennox at a big house near Milton of Campsie, where she'd been since she left school. She was briefly married to another servant, whose name was Mercer – Mum couldn't even remember him. Grandma looked after the Lennox children – nine of them, I think – until the youngest went to boarding school. The Lennoxes pensioned her off quite generously and bought her a small house in Yoker."

"Do you know anything at all about her early life?"

"No. She's never mentioned it. I've never even seen a photograph of her when she was young. I only found out that she came from Millkennet when I got the job here. Mum thought it was a coincidence, and made some remark about Grandma's mother being left almost penniless after her husband was killed in the war."

"Then I wonder who paid the school fees," I said softly. While Shirley had been talking, I'd turned back the faded brown cover of *The Golden Treasury*. Inside was written: *Jean Francis, Form VI, Goldie's Academy 1951-52*. I took the book over to Shirley and laid it on her knee. As she squinted at it without her glasses, a richly dumbfounded expression appeared on her face. "Gobsmacked, aren't you?" I asked gleefully.

Shirley was so shattered she didn't even tick me off for saying "gobsmacked". Lying back in her chair, she closed her eyes and groaned.

It was time, I thought, to tell her about the initials and

the heart. Without mentioning the ghost, I explained how I'd gone with Zak to the Lovers' Tree.

"Zak said *JF* was his granddad's secret love," I said. "I wondered at the time if it could be Grandma, because there must be some reason why Mr Falconer's voice has been haunting us and she's our only link with Millkennet. When I thought her name was Cameron, it seemed I'd got it wrong, but if it was Francis and she went to Goldie's Academy . . . They're the same age, Shirley."

Having already been forced to accept one incredible truth about Grandma, Shirley didn't need convincing.

"It's hard to imagine," she said, wrinkling her nose fastidiously, "but I don't suppose Hugh Falconer has always been as creepy as he is now. And I agree with you – I've thought all along that Grandma must be involved in this business. She's a funny old bird but she loves us dearly, and only something terribly hurtful could keep her away from us all this time. Besides –"

"What?"

"Have you noticed?" asked Shirley, with a dark person's brooding look. "The only quiet times we've known here have been when Grandma was away from home. When she was at Dunoon over Christmas, peace reigned. The very day she flew to Canada, the haunting stopped again."

We looked at each other sombrely in the soft lamplight.

"So do you think –?" I whispered fearfully.

"We'll find out quite soon, won't we?" Shirley sighed.

21

Family Resemblance

On the morning of Tuesday 10 March, Grandma flew into Glasgow Airport. When Shirley and I got home at half-past five, term time at Goldie's Academy was in full swing. Doors slammed, feet ran, voices shrieked and young Hugh Falconer belted out his theme song. Sooty cowered in the kitchen, eyes glaring and hackles raised. Since we'd more than half expected it, our disappointment shouldn't have been so acute. But we'd got so used to normal, peaceful living that the change was hard to bear.

"I'd suggest going to a hotel," Shirley said distractedly, "but my assessments are only half done and I need my computer and God knows how many files. Do you think you can stick it out?"

"No problem," I said reassuringly. "Think what we've stuck out already. It's only ten days till the end of term."

Ten days seemed long, all the same. That very night I dreamt of falling again, and saw Shirley drowning in a deep well. Next day, flashbacks returned me to Goldie's Academy long ago. Looking out of the sitting-room window I saw summer trees, boys playing football and girls in blue tunics sitting in huddles on the grass. I saw Shirley walking hand in hand with the fair boy who wasn't Toby, and foreboding darkened my mind.

Most alarming of all was the reappearance of the ghost. Since she'd seen me with Zak in the park, she seemed angrier and more malevolent than ever. One evening when I was coming upstairs, an empty milk bottle fell through the banisters above and crashed on the step, missing my head by a whisker. When I went to the rubbish chute, a dead pigeon fell from the cupboard roof, shedding mouldy feathers and catching at my jersey with pink, shrivelled claws. The landing light went out without warning and I was pushed violently from behind.

My one comfort was that Shirley didn't know about these incidents. Haggard and preoccupied, she blundered around at home, walking into doors and forgetting to turn off the stove. I admired the way she put aside her troubles at school, bravely putting on an act for her pupils, but I knew she was near the end of her tether. I couldn't wait to escape to school in the morning and it was there, strangely and unexpectedly, that the mystery began to unwind.

On Thursday afternoon, our last lesson was History. We had just finished a module on the Jacobites and it was time for Granny Clark to announce something new.

"Our next topic is 'Education in Millkennet'," she said, writing the words in large letters on the board. "There have been schools in Millkennet for six hundred years, so it'll be a very interesting study indeed."

There was a growl of disapproval. Most people in our class only liked History when it was about William Wallace and Robert the Bruce, and us mashing the English at the Battle of Bannockburn.

"Aw, no, Miss! Tell us a story," they begged. "Tell us about Wallace the Bruce."

Granny's Adam's apple swelled visibly.

"No, trust me, you'll enjoy this," she said, rolling her amethyst eye over the class. "Well, some of you will," she added more truthfully.

Granny was a realistic teacher. Our class was divided into groups. Those who could read and write got grown-up worksheets. Those who couldn't got easier ones with plenty of drawing and colouring in. My group was given a big box labelled *Goldie's Academy 1875-1986*. It was full of old school magazines, exercise books, registers, exam papers and thick photograph albums.

"I suggest you browse through the box today," Granny said. "Get a feel of what's there and we'll start the worksheets on Tuesday."

Which was how, at 2.30 on a cold March afternoon, I began to turn the pages of a dusty old photograph album. Shiny black and white photographs had been fixed at the corners with little paper triangles and information written in ink underneath. *Rugby First XV 1951: Hockey First XI 1952.* Boys in boots and striped jerseys, girls in braided tunics and short-sleeved shirts – familiar, yet fixed in history as firmly as Robert the Bruce. It was both disturbing and bewitching in our humdrum, modern classroom, to find myself gazing at Shirley, with her black hair swooping around her vivid, intelligent face. Her dark eyes looked serenely into mine, her full mouth turned up at the corners in a secretive, happy smile.

Only of course, it wasn't Shirley. It was Grandma. *School Prefects 1951-1952. Front row, left to right: Alan Macbeth, Jean Francis . . .* I suppose it was silly of me to be so amazed. I'd heard it said time and again how like Grandma Shirley was. But, except occasionally when Shirley frowned at me over her specs, I'd seen no resemblance between the dark, beautiful young woman and the white-haired, sharp-nosed old one. Even after I'd learned that Grandma had gone to Goldie's, the truth hadn't occurred to me.

"Mrs Clark," I said breathlessly as Granny paused by my chair, "this is my grandma."

When Granny peered over my shoulder, she saw the resemblance, all right.

"Good heavens, isn't that amazing?" she laughed. "And look, Alice." She ran her forefinger along the row of smiling teenagers. "Your grandma must have been at school with Mr and Mrs Falconer."

I felt as if icy water was trickling down my back. As I followed the pointing finger, all but three of the faces in the photograph went out of focus. Appalled but fascinated, I gazed at the young people I'd seen in the memorial garden, and on the steps of Goldie's Academy. They were fair, blue-eyed Hugh Falconer and the two women in his life, dark-haired Jean Francis whom he'd loved and Rosalie Jordan, the redhead he'd married. She was Zak Petersen's grandmother who had died in August – *the ghost on our stair.* I was still staring and shivering as the period bell shrilled through the school.

On the way to the cloakroom with the other girls, I made a big effort and got myself together. I was due at the chess club, but I'd no time for that. When I'd collected my fleece from my locker, I went back to the History room. Granny Clark was sitting at her desk, marking exercise books and drinking coffee from a plastic cup.

"Mrs Clark," I said, trying to keep my voice casual, "is it OK if I look again at the photograph album with Grandma in it?"

Granny smiled at me. She could be quite nice sometimes.

"Help yourself. It's still on the table," she said. "I didn't know your grandma went to Goldie's, Alice."

"Neither did I, until recently," I replied.

In the empty classroom I sat turning over the thick, acrid pages. I saw Grandma as captain of girls' tennis. I saw her as Olivia in *Twelfth Night.* I saw her playing a violin in Goldie's Academy string quartet. As I looked my sense of mystery deepened. What on earth had happened to turn this vibrant girl into an elderly woman who did nothing but watch sport on television and work once a week in the Oxfam shop? Shaking my head, I turned to the last photograph in the book.

Dux of the School, Jean Francis: Runner-up, Hugh Falconer: County Sports Champion, Rosalie Jordan . . .

Between the couple who had become Mr and Mrs Hugh Falconer, Jean Francis stood with a medal pinned to her lapel and a bundle of prize books in the crook of her right arm. The happy smile of her earlier photographs was gone, and she looked at the camera with a wary, bewildered expression so familiar that it made me want to cry. Then I noticed that she'd had an accident. Her blazer was pulled loosely over her shoulder because her left arm was in a sling.

Hugh Falconer wasn't smiling either. His confident grin had been replaced by the melancholy, haunted look I'd seen on his face on Burns Night, when he gazed at Jean Francis's granddaughter.

Ae fond kiss, and then we sever!
Ae fareweel, alas, for ever . . .

Only Rosalie Jordan was happy, but it wasn't the kind of happiness you'd have wanted to share. Narrow-eyed and sharp-toothed, she was grinning like a well-fed tiger. With a jolt of terror, I saw another family resemblance which had escaped me. This was how Zak had smiled at me in the school corridor, the day he'd threatened to punish me by hurting Shirley.

That was when, looking at my injured grandmother, I realised that I had made a terrible mistake. If the ghost of Rosalie Jordan hated me, it was only because I was related to someone else. The granddaughter who looked like Jean Francis was her real prey.

Despite my fear, my mind worked coolly. Right now Shirley would be rehearsing her choir in the music department. If I went there at once and waited, I could catch her as she came out. I would tell her – what? That she was in danger from a ghost she'd never seen? That I'd changed my mind and wanted to go to a hotel straight away? In a way it didn't matter, since from now on I'd be sticking to her even more closely than she'd been sticking to me. I was pulling on my fleece when the classroom door opened and Mrs Liddell, who was also an English teacher, came in.

"Mrs Clark, excuse me," she said. "It's Alice I want – I've been looking for her everywhere. Alice, Shirley has a bad headache and we persuaded her to leave early. She says you mustn't worry, but just go home when you're ready –"

I didn't wait to hear any more. Leaving my bag on the classroom floor, I ran into the corridor. Then I just kept on running.

22

The Evil Day

I'd taken my keys out of my pocket as I pounded down Corngate but, when I panted into the yard at Goldie Court, I saw that the door at the bottom of our stair was open. As I bounded upwards I could smell the ghost's mouldy aroma and feel frost stinging my sweating skin. Crashing onto the landing, I saw that the apartment door was also open. Shirley, still in the green skirt and blouse she'd worn to school, was pressing her back to the wall outside. Her hair was in disarray, her eyes unnaturally bright and wide.

The ghost had her back to me. She kept making mean little pouncing movements towards Shirley, who twitched involuntarily, each time shifting a little further away from the shelter of the door. I was so furious at this cruel baiting that I made a very bad move.

"Shirley!" I screamed, running to try to shield her and leaving the top of the stair unguarded.

As I jumped forward, the ghost whipped round, her face twisted and her hands extended like claws. I tried to

142

duck past her and reach Shirley, but a force like an electric shock sent me spinning through our open door. As I scrambled to my feet, I saw the ghost grab Shirley, gripping her frail body with monstrous strength. Shirley was lifted like a drift of leaves in the wind, whirled across the landing and thrown violently down the stair. In the instant when I heard her body thud onto the hall floor, I was aware of Sooty going loco in the kitchen. Somehow, as the phantom turned snarling to me, I had the presence of mind to dive and kick open the kitchen door.

With his eyes glaring and his claws unsheathed, Sooty launched himself onto the landing. Spitting like a cobra, he tore at the ghost in a frenzy of hatred and revenge. I heard a thin, unearthly scream and witnessed some foul disintegration, like an explosion of milk and copper leaves. Then there was emptiness and a silence like death.

With my heart in my throat, I ran downstairs and knelt beside my sister. She was lying on her left side with her arm twisted beneath her. Her eyes were closed and there was blood trickling from a gash on her forehead and from her nose. *Remember now thy Creator in the days of thy youth, when the evil days come not* . . . No, not so. The evil days had come for me in my youth, and this was the worst. When Mum and Dad had died, I'd had Grandma and Shirley with me. Now Shirley was dead too, and I was completely alone.

I was vaguely aware of someone running downstairs and crouching beside me. It was Mrs Huntly from next door.

"Don't try to move her," she warned me. "I'll phone for an ambulance." I was afraid even to touch Shirley. I went on kneeling on the floor, too numb to pray, too bereft to cry. Soon Mrs Huntly came back. "The ambulance is on its way," she said. "Oh, Alice, I'm so sorry, but I can't come with you. My little boy's sick and my husband isn't home. As soon as he gets back, one of us will come."

"Oh, yes," I whispered vaguely. "Thank you."

The ambulance arrived quite soon. Two men in green fluorescent coats came into the hall. As I moved aside they eased Shirley onto her back, put a collar round her neck and strapped her left arm to her chest. They brought a stretcher and lifted her onto it, covering her with a red blanket. When they put her into the ambulance, I got in too. As we were rushed away with the siren wailing like grief, the most idiotic thought came into my mind. If Shirley was dead, she wouldn't be able to see me getting my Geography prize.

But Shirley wasn't dead. As the ambulance sped towards Stirling, she began to come round. Her eyelids fluttered and her right hand crept out from under the blanket. I covered it with mine.

"Alice."

"Yes, darling. I'm here."

"Are we in an ambulance?"

"Yes."

There was a little pause, then Shirley said clearly, "Listen. When we get to the hospital, you must phone Grandma. Tell her – this time she's got to come."

"Right. I've got the change from my dinner money. Don't worry about a thing."

I went on holding her hand until the ambulance swung into the hospital yard. As the doors were pinned back, Shirley opened her eyes.

"Wait for me," she said. "We must go home together."

I tried to run along beside the trolley, but the orderlies outstripped me. A long, brightly lit corridor swallowed Shirley, and I was left in a reception hall with a sweet, antiseptic smell. It had sugar-pink walls, a long desk with glass partitions and a lot of imitation leather chairs. A young nurse came with a clipboard and made me sit down.

"Are you with the patient who just came in?" she asked kindly.

"My sister," I nodded.

"Tell me her full name."

"Shirley Jean Fairlie."

"Address?"

"27 Knightshill Avenue – no, sorry, that's not right. 2 Goldie Court, Millkennet."

"How old is she?"

"Twenty-seven."

"When's her birthday?"

"Fifteenth of August."

The nurse subtracted and wrote down Shirley's date of birth.

"Who's her next of kin?" she asked.

"What? Oh, me, I suppose."

The nurse patted my knee.

"Of course you are," she agreed, "but isn't there someone older in the family?"

"My grandma. She lives in Glasgow. I'm going to phone her," I said.

The nurse nodded.

"Good idea. There's a pay-phone in the corridor," she told me. "Go and ring her now, and I'll get you a cup of tea."

I lifted the phone shakily, fumbling as I put in twenty pence and dialled Grandma's number. It rang and rang and rang, but she didn't answer. The nurse brought me a cup of weak, sweet liquid that seemed to have absorbed the antiseptic smell. When I'd taken a few sips, I abandoned it and went back to the phone. There was still no reply.

There was a clock on the wall above the reception desk. The time was five-forty. At five-fifty, I rang Grandma again. Three calls later, at half-past six, I began to despair. Shrinking into a chair in a corner, I watched the red second hand move leisurely round the clock's bland face. Minutes ticked icily by.

Doctors and nurses passed and I was dimly aware of other patients coming in; walking wounded with patched eyes and bleeding hands, a young man on a trolley, a child screaming in his mother's arms. It was awful, but I had no sympathy to spare for them, I had so much trouble of my own. Had Grandma gone away again without telling us? Would Shirley be allowed to come home? If she was, how was I going to look after her? Who would look after me? Someone brought me another cup of tea.

At half-past seven I tried Grandma's number again. When she didn't answer, I gave up hope.

It was just after eight when a young doctor in a white coat came along the corridor and approached me.

"Are you Alice Fairlie?"

"Yes."

"Right, Alice. We've finished treating your sister now. She has a fractured elbow and a broken wrist, and I'm afraid by tomorrow she's going to feel very stiff and sore. We wanted to keep her here overnight, but she won't hear of it. Perhaps if you –"

"Please," I interrupted impatiently, "I just want to see her."

The doctor jerked his thumb.

"Along there. Last door on the left," he said.

I pelted down the corridor and opened the door. Shirley was huddled in a chair by an unoccupied bed. She had a dressing taped to her forehead and her left arm, encased in plaster from her fingers to her shoulder, was in a sling. I'd been determined to be strong, but as I ran towards her I burst into tears. When she realised that I hadn't been able to contact Grandma, she began to cry too. We were snivelling and passing each other paper handkerchiefs when something miraculous happened. The door flew open and, in a dramatic swish of long black skirts, Grandma strode into the room. She gave me a strong hug and touched Shirley more tenderly.

"Well, you two!" she scolded. "Can I not leave you alone for ten minutes without you getting yourselves into a pickle?"

This was outrageous, but Shirley and I were too dumbfounded to protest. Seeing our amazement, Grandma briskly explained.

"You have good neighbours. When Mrs Huntly went to lock up your place, she sensibly looked in your telephone book for an emergency contact. As soon as she rang me I got a taxi, then a train from Queen Street. Mr Huntly met me at Stirling station, and he's waiting outside to take us home."

I was so relieved that I started whimpering again. Needless to say, I got short shrift.

"Stop that at once," ordered Grandma. "You're not hurt, are you? Now, Shirley girl, can you walk or shall I get someone to bring a wheelchair?"

Shirley looked deeply offended. Gritting her teeth, she levered herself onto her feet and put her free hand on my shoulder. I put my arm round her waist and we began to walk slowly towards the door.

23

Indiscretion

For all her bossiness, it was wonderful having Grandma at home with us. While she undressed Shirley and put her to bed I scooted round, making up a spare bed in the study, fetching extra pillows for Shirley and brewing tea. I made myself a huge helping of toasted cheese and was washing it down with Coke when Grandma came into the kitchen.

"I want to see Shirley," I said.

I could see her opening her mouth to say no, but then she relented.

"All right, but only for a few minutes. She's very tired."

Shirley was lying propped up on pillows, her black hair tumbling over her patched forehead. She opened her eyes when she heard me and tapped her forefinger on the duvet at her undamaged side. When I sat down gingerly, she took my hand lightly in hers.

"Well, Mousie," she said feebly, "here's a fine to-do. Thank you for trying to help me. It was very brave when you must have been so frightened."

I shook my head regretfully.

"I was stupid," I said. "If only I'd dashed past the ghost and let Sooty out of the kitchen, he'd have got to her before she got to you."

I could see Shirley struggling to make sense of this in her aching head.

"I don't understand. How do you mean?" she asked.

"After the ghost threw you downstairs, I heard Sooty yowling, so I let him out," I explained. "He went for her tooth and nail. It was gruesome, but he did for her, once and for all. She won't come haunting here again." I suppose being keyed up and overtired made me indiscreet. When Shirley didn't respond, I foolishly gabbled on. "Sooty's always hated the ghost, ever since the day in November when he saw her from the kitchen window. The day he trashed the sitting-room, he'd seen her in the park . . . aaa-rgh."

Too late I realised my error and faltered to a halt. As appalled understanding dawned, Shirley withdrew her hand sharply from mine.

"Are you telling me," she said slowly, "that you've seen that nightmare creature before?"

There was no point in denying it now.

"Yes," I admitted. "Quite often, actually."

Shirley was the least violent person on earth, but I think if she could have struck me then, she would.

"You stupid, stupid child," she hissed furiously. "Why didn't you tell me?"

I went stiff with indignation.

"Because," I replied haughtily, "I thought *you* couldn't

see her. You never mentioned her, and on the night when we came back from Loch Lomond you walked straight past her on the landing. I knew you'd seen the school and the war memorial, but apart from that I reckoned you only heard noises. I thought you had enough to put up with, without knowing I could see a ghost you couldn't see."

Beads of perspiration were breaking on Shirley's forehead and flowing down her face.

"Couldn't see?" she repeated despairingly. "I thought you couldn't see her. You seemed so stoical and matter-of-fact. I honestly believed you'd be safe here till Easter – and that afterwards you would be free."

"You mean, we would be free," I corrected her.

"No." Shirley wiped her wet face clumsily with her wrist. "Since Grandma came back from Canada, I haven't believed I could escape. I've been sure that wherever I went that cruel spectre would be with me, tormenting me till I died. Today when the doorbell rang and I was dragged onto the landing, I thought it was all over. If I hadn't been so afraid of leaving you alone, I'd have been glad." She licked her dry lips, then burst out reproachfully, "Oh, God, Alice – how could you do this to me? I've been so careful. I've hardly let you out of my sight for fear you'd even glimpse her and not have me to turn to. Don't you understand? What she did to me, she could have done to you."

Shirley was in a dreadful state, moaning and plucking at the duvet with her fingers. I was shocked rigid – and very scared.

"Shirley," I pleaded, "calm down. She wouldn't have done it to me because it was you she wanted to hurt. I think she did the same once before, to Grandma." I don't know if Shirley heard me. She was shivering and her hand wouldn't keep still. "Oh, please, cool it," I begged. "If old Thunderface comes in here, I'm dead."

This bald statement got through to her. She closed her hand and forced an unconvincing smile.

"Very likely," she agreed. "Go to bed then, Alice."

I really thought I'd done my best, and this curt dismissal was so hurtful that I walked out without saying goodnight. It was only long afterwards that Shirley explained to me why she'd felt so bitter. That night, she said, when she was at her lowest point, I had taken away from her the one thing she was proud of. She had believed that by always being there for me, she was protecting me from the worst of the horrors that were menacing her. Even when she was lying badly injured on a hospital trolley, she'd only been scared that I might have to go back to Goldie Court without her. I felt terrible, but of course by then she had long since forgiven me.

I'd had a shower and I was in bed, trying unsuccessfully to relax with a teen magazine, when Grandma appeared suddenly. She twitched the mag out of my hand, examined it scornfully and dropped it into the waste-paper basket. Then she sat down on the end of my bed.

"You don't have to get up early," she told me. "I've just spoken to your form mistress, Mrs Clark. What a delightful person! I've broken the news about Shirley and said that you won't be at school tomorrow either."

"Why won't I?"

"Because I say so. Now lie down."

It was oddly reassuring to be ordered about and I snuggled down obediently. Grandma tucked my duvet round me and gave me a kiss.

"Good night, sleep tight," she said.

So much had happened since my History class in the afternoon, I'd almost forgotten the photographs of Jean Francis. Now their strangeness flooded back to me and, in the moment when Grandma switched off my lamp, I saw for the first time in her old face the softer features of her youth. As she was about to shut the door, I called her back.

"Grandma!"

"What now?"

"I wonder why I never noticed until today how alike you and Shirley are?"

Grandma snorted.

"Because," she replied tartly, "children never look at their grandmothers. They're too busy looking at young, beautiful people, like themselves."

You had to hand it to her. She might have stopped reading books, but she was still quite bright.

24

Cats Out of Bags

Although I hadn't set my alarm, I began waking up at my usual time. For a few minutes I lay warm and content, with only the tiniest flicker of awareness that this wasn't an ordinary morning. There was a kind of explosion in my mind as I remembered everything. Getting up quickly, I put on my dressing-gown and went into the hall. Shirley's door was ajar but the room was in darkness. There was a light on in the kitchen, so I went in.

Grandma, also in her dressing-gown, was sitting at the table with a cup of coffee. She looked completely bushed and I reckoned she'd been up all night. I fetched myself a coffee and sat down.

"How's Shirley?" I asked.

Grandma shrugged helplessly.

"I really don't know," she said. "She's sleeping now, but she's had a very bad night – not surprisingly since she's in a lot of pain. But there's more wrong than that."

"How do you mean?" I inquired with caution.

Grandma ran her hand through her thick white hair, in a gesture that was pure Shirley.

"At first I thought she was delirious," she told me, "but although her temperature was high, it wasn't high enough for that. She kept falling asleep then starting awake a moment later, crying that a red-haired girl had pushed her downstairs. Alice –" Grandma's eyes held mine darkly "– what on earth has been going on here? When I saw Shirley yesterday, she looked so ill I hardly recognised her. Did someone push her downstairs?"

I had kept the truth from Shirley and I hadn't been thanked for it. Besides, nobody could hold out on Grandma for long. So I told her everything: how the giggles and whispers had risen to the full-scale racket of a school; how we'd both been frightened by a ghostly schoolgirl but hadn't told each other; how we'd heard a boy's voice singing *Ae Fond Kiss*; how ghost trains had rattled by.

"I kept seeing Shirley in a Goldie's Academy uniform," I said, "only now I know it wasn't Shirley, it was you. I know Hugh Falconer carved your initials on the Lovers' Tree and I know who the ghost was who tried to kill Shirley. Her name was Rosalie Jordan."

It was the only time in my life that I've ever seen Grandma totally gobsmacked. Her mouth was like an O and her eyes goggled like a frog's. She kept gulping, then suddenly she dropped her head into her hands.

"Oh, my poor bairns," she whispered. "What have I done to you? This is all my fault."

"Don't be daft, Grandma," I said, mildly impatient. "How could it be your fault?"

When she raised her head, it was plain that some awful thought had struck Grandma.

"Alice," she gasped, "does Shirley know I went to Goldie's Academy?"

I admit I had trouble repressing a grin.

"Yip," I said briskly. "It was written in a book you gave her. But she doesn't know who the ghost was, or about you getting the dux medal. *Yet*," I couldn't resist adding.

Grandma looked slightly relieved, but then her expression turned shifty.

"You mentioned Hugh Falconer," she said, trying unsuccessfully to sound casual. "Tell me, has Shirley ever met Hugh Falconer?"

"Grandma," I said with relish, "Hugh Falconer is Shirley's boss."

I honestly thought she was going to blow a fuse, but just then Shirley cried out fretfully from her bed.

"Grandma! Where are you?"

Grandma gnashed her teeth. Gulping down some coffee, she staggered to her feet.

"Don't tell Shirley anything she doesn't already know," she ordered. "I'll explain everything later. All right, my love, I'm coming," she called, as Shirley's querulous voice sounded again.

I had every intention of disobeying Grandma. Apart from wanting to see Shirley's face when she heard that Grandma had won a dux medal, I also thought she should know that cats were emerging from bags at an alarming rate. Sneaking past Grandma, however, was as hard as outwitting a dragon. By the time she'd thrown on her clothes she was back in stroppy mode and, whenever I approached Shirley's door, she pounced. At nine o'clock I was told to get my coat on, because I was going shopping.

"There's no food in this house," Grandma complained.

"There are pizzas in the freezer," I told her.

"That's what I mean," she said.

While she was poking about in the larder and writing a long shopping list, I at last managed to slip into Shirley's room. She was looking wrecked, the skin around her mouth grey and her eyes far too large for her face. But she smiled at me through her tangled hair, so I went and sat beside her.

"You look terrible," I whispered.

"Thank you. I feel terrible," Shirley whispered back. "Is this an unofficial visit?"

"Too right," I replied. "I just wanted to warn you. She knows everything."

Shirley's eyes became even larger.

"What?" she breathed incredulously. "You didn't tell her, did you?"

"No," I said. "You did. You've been blabbing in the night."

"Oh, God!" Shirley grimaced and closed her eyes, but then she waved her hand languidly. "Well, never mind," she said. "The fevered brain, you know. She won't believe a word of it."

"Oh, but she does," I contradicted. "She says it's all her fault and she's going to explain everything later."

"She certainly has a lot of explaining to do," Shirley said.

I reckoned that, unless Grandma was going to hire a truck, the shopping list must be nearly complete.

"I've more to tell," I said mysteriously, "so I'll speak to you later. Right now I'm going out to buy lashings of cream, jam roly-polies and a tonne of butter. You're going to be fattened up."

"And you're going to be thinned down," snapped Grandma behind me. "Get out of here this minute. The shopping list's on the table."

As things turned out, I didn't have another chance to speak to Shirley alone. When I staggered back with the shopping, a doctor was with her. He had come to check that the plaster cast wasn't stopping her circulation but, when he'd examined her, he gave her a pain-killing injection. Twenty minutes later, she was asleep.

When Shirley woke again, it was after five o'clock. I put clean bedclothes on her bed while Grandma helped her to bath. Since Grandma usually treated Shirley and me as if we were five years old, her nannying skills were proving useful. Pity about the chippy manner, but life's rarely perfect. But because I couldn't tell her about the photographs, especially the one of Grandma with her arm broken, the story we heard later in the evening was even more shocking to Shirley than it was to me.

25

Schoolgirls

"I've never imagined telling my story to anyone," Grandma said, "but you've suffered because of me and I owe you the truth. You're kind girls, and, when you know everything, I don't think you'll judge me harshly."

Grandma was sitting where she'd sat on and off for years, in an old Victorian chair that Shirley had brought from Knightshill Avenue. Shirley, looking much better after her long sleep, was in bed and I was perched on a stool between them. Each way I looked I saw the same face, pale, dark-eyed and serious. Grandma folded her long hands in her lap, considered for a moment, then began.

"My father, Cameron Francis, was a carpenter in Millkennet. He was a skilled worker, but he'd lived through hard times and known the insecurity of being unemployed. He wanted a better life for his children and saw a good education as the way to achieve it.

"In the year war broke out, when I was five and my sister Alice only a few months old, he entered our names for Goldie's Academy, although I doubt he'd even begun to think how he'd pay the fees. In 1940 he enlisted in the army and a year later he was dead, blown to pieces in the Libyan desert. My mother was left with two young children and only one ambition – to educate us in the way he'd wanted.

"From then on, the sole object of her life was to save money. We moved from our house in Victoria Road to a tenement flat in Pennyhill and my mother went out to work. She scrubbed floors in the hospital during the day and washed dishes at a hotel at night, while I sat at my books and looked after my little sister. Even so, I don't think she could have afforded Goldie's if I hadn't won a scholarship when I was eleven, which covered my fees for six years. My mother paid for my uniform and my books, and went on saving for Alice."

I looked at Shirley to see how she was taking this, but her face was impassive. Perhaps she thought she was beyond surprise.

"Did you like Goldie's Academy, Grandma?" I asked.

"Yes, I loved it," Grandma smiled. "Later in life I came to disapprove of privilege in education, but at the time I was just glad to be there. It was a lovely school, friendly and unsnobbish and great fun, even if the lavatories stank and naughty boys were whacked occasionally. The teaching was excellent and I was a good pupil. I learned Latin and Greek and decided that I'd be an archaeologist when I grew up. Indeed, there was only ever one problem."

"Which was?"

"A fly in the ointment of life," said Grandma with a wry smile. "In my class there was a girl called Rosalie Jordan." I knew the name meant nothing to Shirley but, as Grandma continued, I saw her move uneasily on her pillows. "Rosalie wasn't exactly pretty, but she had the most amazing hair – thick and curly and the colour of a barn on fire. She was the kind of child who can charm adults but is vile to other children. There was never any point in complaining about her, because teachers thought she was sweet. She was horrid to everyone in the class, but the worst of her venom was reserved for me – partly because she thought I was a slum child and partly because I had a bad habit of winning the prizes she coveted. And of course –" Grandma's lips twitched in self-mockery "– I wasn't always the stroppy old bat I am now. Indeed, I was quite popular. Anyway, the little pig couldn't pass my desk without knocking over my ink bottle and, if I ever left my blazer in the cloakroom, when I came back she'd cut a hole in it."

"Who does that recall?" interrupted Shirley, looking at me.

"The ghost was Zak's grandmother," I told her, remembering with a shudder how the weird creature had wept over him in the park.

"Yes, I know that," said Shirley, surprising me. "She'd always reminded me of someone, but I couldn't think who until that last Saturday when Zak came round. He was in the sitting-room banging on about something, when it suddenly occurred to me what was wrong with his face."

161

"What was that?"

"No one with blond hair should have bright red eyebrows," Shirley said. "I realised that before he dyed his hair he must've been a dead ringer for the ghost. I was so spooked I walked out on him. What did you say the ghost's name was, Grandma?"

"Rosalie Jordan. Shall I go on?"

"Yes. Sorry."

"By the time we got to the upper school," Grandma said, "I had won another prize Rosalie coveted – the attention of Hugh Falconer. I don't suppose Hugh is glamorous now –" she glanced furtively at Shirley, who maintained a stony look "– but fifty years ago he was very desirable. He was also clever – not as clever as I was myself, but we enjoyed and laughed at the same things. Rosalie was madly jealous; her father and Hugh's were partners in the same legal firm and she'd grown up thinking Hugh was hers by right. She sniffed around after us like a bloodhound and –" Grandma frowned, choosing her words "– the virulence of her envy began to unnerve me. I knew she'd harm me if she could."

Shirley shivered.

"That's how I felt," she said. "Once I got used to it, nothing else in the haunting terrified me. The noises were wearisome but not threatening. It was strange to see Alice riding her bike along Corngate and slinking about at the hall door because she was late for prayers, but I couldn't be frightened by Alice. The ghost was something else. Until – what happened yesterday – she never really came close to me, but the intensity of her hatred scared me half to death. I tried to ignore her but I knew she'd get me in the end."

"You should've done what I did," I said. "Stuck out your tongue, thumbed your nose and said, 'Yah – boo, Ginger!' It didn't scare her, but it made me feel a hell of a lot better."

Grandma, who had looked appalled at Shirley's words, smiled faintly.

"She must have found that like old times," she said, touching my hair. "My little sister Alice came to Goldie's when I was in the fifth form. You're as like her as Shirley is like me. She's still proud of the way she plagued Rosalie. Alice," she added with fond amusement, "always thought her main task in life was to fight my battles for me."

Shirley gave me the most affectionate smile I'd had from her since she came back from the hospital.

"That sounds familiar," she said. "Maybe that's why the ghost never came into the apartment. She was scared of you."

"Scared of Sooty, if she had any sense," I replied.

Grandma twisted her thin wedding ring round her finger and went on with her story.

"Unfortunately," she said, "a situation arose that even Alice couldn't protect me from. In my final year at Goldie's I won a bursary – that's what a scholarship was called in those days – to St Andrews University to study Classics. Hugh and Rosalie had applied for places at St Andrews too, but Rosalie failed her exams and her parents decided to send her to school abroad. I'm sure the thought of Hugh and me together at University brought her to the brink of madness, then she got wind of something that pushed her right over. On the day when the prize list was announced and she heard that I had won the dux medal, she waited for me on the top landing. She was an immensely strong girl, and when I came out of the cloakroom she grabbed me. I was lifted as if I was a bundle of straw and hurled down the stair."

Shirley had looked more perplexed than distressed as the extent of Grandma's brilliance was revealed, but now she cried out sharply.

"Oh, no! Not you too!"

Grandma leant over and kindly patted her hand.

"There, there, my girl," she soothed, "don't get upset. I broke my arm and banged my head, but it could have been much, much worse."

"You mean, she might have killed you," I agreed soberly.

Grandma looked at me earnestly, then she looked at Shirley, then she lay back in the chair and closed her eyes.

"No. She might have killed my baby," she said.

26

Jean's Story

Just for a moment, there was a silence so profound that I thought I could hear my own heart beat. Shirley and I glanced warily at each other, then we stared at Grandma. She was sitting with her eyes screwed up, as if she were afraid that when she opened them she would see anger or censure on our faces. I'm proud that when she did dare to look at us, she saw nothing of the kind.

"Was it my mum?" I whispered.

Grandma nodded. She groped for her handkerchief and blew her nose, then went on steadily.

"Hugh Falconer and I fell in love when we were fourteen," she said. "We shared a desk and walked in the park and held hands when our teachers weren't looking. We went dancing on Saturday nights and Hugh carved our initials on the Lovers' Tree. Only by the time we were in the sixth form, we'd gone far beyond holding hands and exchanging kisses after the dance. We first made love in the Aiken Glen on a September night, and after that we couldn't get enough of each other. Until winter came we made love in the glen, then we made love in the Falconers' summerhouse. It seems crazy now, but there was no sex education then and I was incredibly ill-informed. Hugh said he was being careful and I trusted him.

"In April, when we sat the bursary examinations, I missed a period. I thought I was just stressed because so much depended on my doing well, but when I missed again in May, I was apprehensive. By June, I knew I was pregnant."

"Oh, poor Grandma," whispered Shirley sympathetically. "Whatever did you do?"

Grandma gave her a grateful glance.

"I asked Hugh to meet me in the memorial garden one evening," she replied, "and I told him about the baby. Naturally, he was upset, but he told me not to worry, that he would sort something out. I never knew whether he told Rosalie, or whether yet again she'd been snooping round after us. But it was certainly the next day when she arranged for me to have an accident."

"Without witnesses," I said angrily.

Grandma almost smiled.

"Not exactly," she said. "There was one witness, Euclid the school cat. He flew at Rosalie and scratched her arms, which was obliging, since I'd never been able to stand him."

I avoided Shirley's eye.

"What happened then?" I prompted.

"I was determined to take my prizes," Grandma said, with a proud tilt of her chin, "because I'd earned them.

But I'd made up my mind that afterwards I'd go home and tell my mother the truth. I knew there would be a terrible scene – she'd worked her fingers to the bone to educate me and the labour had made her bitter and hard. I knew she didn't really love me; what she'd done was partly a tribute to my dead father, but also partly an insurance for herself. The trade-off was that if she educated us, Alice and I would provide for her later on. Since in those days I couldn't possibly go to University with a baby and Alice was still very young, it was the end of a dream for her too. Even so, I didn't really anticipate her reaction."

Shirley was looking exhausted again and she was holding her arm as if it hurt badly.

"How did she react?" she asked fearfully.

Grandma sighed.

"It's difficult for young people living in a tolerant age to understand how most people thought fifty years ago," she said. "To have a baby with a man you weren't married to was considered a deep disgrace. In my mother's eyes, I'd demolished everything she'd slaved for and shamed my family. It didn't matter how often I said, 'Hugh will marry me,' she couldn't cope. When she'd finished slapping me round the head and calling me names I'd never heard before, she said, 'Let him marry you or let him keep you, for you're no daughter of mine.' Then she told me to pack a bag and get out of the house. I remember Alice crying and putting things in a suitcase for me, because I couldn't do it with one hand. I could still hear her howling as I walked down Pennyhill. The irony was, I was still wearing my school uniform with the dux medal pinned to my lapel."

167

This was too much for Shirley. She put her hand over her face and began to sob bitterly. Grandma got up in a hurry.

"Now, now, my pet, don't cry," she murmured, taking Shirley's head between her hands as if the twenty-seven-year-old woman was a little child of long ago. "This is ancient history. Anyway," she added briskly, as if she'd come to a convenient break in a bedtime story, "that's enough for tonight. I'll tell you the rest tomorrow."

I was aghast and Shirley said vehemently, "No! I'll try not to cry, but please – you must tell us now."

Grandma looked uncertain, but when she'd given Shirley two pills and held a glass of water to her lips, she sat down again.

"All right. I went to the Falconers' house in Corngate, because I didn't know where else to go. I should have been warned, because Hugh had been avoiding me, but it wasn't till he came downstairs that I read my future in his face. He said Rosalie had warned his parents that I was claiming falsely that he had fathered my child, and that his father had advised him to deny everything. He muttered that he was dependent on his parents financially, and that I couldn't expect him to sacrifice University and a good career because he'd made one foolish mistake. He said he was sorry, then he shut the door.

"My first instinct was to go and jump in the river, but just then fate intervened. While I was standing weeping in Corngate, my friend Mary McLeod drove by with her mother. Mary's father was a minister and she'd been my best friend since primary school. When she saw me, Mrs McLeod stopped the car and made me get in. I was pretty incoherent, but she got the gist and took me home with her."

"Is that Mary at Dunoon?" I asked.

"Yes," Grandma said. "She's a retired GP, as kind a person as her mother. Mrs McLeod listened to my story and said I should tell her who the baby's father was, but I wouldn't and she accepted that. She explained what I already knew, that I must give up hope of University and a career, then she said she thought she could help me. I stayed a week with her while she arranged for me to go to her niece Mrs Lennox, who was married to a wealthy businessman and lived in a big house at Milton of Campsie. I was to help with the children – there were two at that time – in return for board and lodging and a small wage. The best of it was that Mrs Lennox would look after me and let me keep my child. Valerie was born and brought up with the little Lennoxes. She went to school in Kirkintilloch and then into nursing, and grew up the best daughter a woman ever had." Grandma smiled a secret, loving smile. "I even found a use for my dux medal," she told us. "When Valerie got engaged to your father, I sold it to buy her wedding dress."

"What a lovely idea," said Shirley softly. "I have the dress safely laid away. I'm keeping it for Alice."

I was opening my mouth to say who I wanted to wear the dress first, but Grandma gave me a warning look, so I shut it again.

"Who was Mr Mercer?" I asked instead.

For an instant, Grandma really looked as if she couldn't remember, but then she said, "His name was John. He was Mr Lennox's chauffeur – a decent, kind young man who didn't seem to mind that I already had a child. He was good to me, but I really only married him to be Mrs Somebody for Valerie's sake. He died suddenly two years later, and the dreadful thing is that now I hardly ever think about him."

"Did Mum know that he wasn't really her father?" I inquired curiously.

"Yes," Grandma replied. "When Valerie was twelve, the Lennoxes were going to take her on holiday with them to Norway, and she needed a passport. We had to send her birth certificate and I told her then – simply that her father was a boy I'd been at school with. She gave me a hug and said it didn't matter, because she'd only ever needed me. She said it would be our secret and, although I assume she told your father, not another word was ever said."

"What I don't understand," sniffed Shirley, getting tearful again, "is why you never told *me* the truth. When I think of the awful things Dad used to say, and how I thought you and I had no interests in common, I feel ashamed. But what was I to think? When I got my scholarship you never said you were proud of me, and you wouldn't come to my graduation. Why did you deceive me?"

This question obviously upset Grandma.

"Shirley," she said earnestly, "I never meant to deceive you. As you know well, things happen to us that are almost impossible to talk about, especially to those we love. Besides, by the time you were born, I'd spent twenty years bringing up children, changing their nappies, wiping their noses, nursing them through chickenpox, caring for them when they fell off ponies and broke their arms and legs. When do you think I had time to read new books or even think about old ones? I'd left my violin at Pennyhill and by the time I was thirty I could have written all the Greek I remembered on the back of a stamp. I wasn't unhappy. The Lennoxes were good to me, and your mother was worth far more than anything I'd lost. But even before I retired to Yoker, I'd become what your father thought I was, an ignorant old person.

"Of course I was proud of you when you got your scholarship. It was David and Valerie's pride that worried me. You were such a sensitive, conscientious child, I was afraid you'd be crushed by their expectations. As for your graduation – I'm sorry you were hurt, but I couldn't bear to go to St Andrews. I was jealous, Shirley. Try to understand."

For a moment, I thought I was going to have them both blubbing all over me. I coughed disapprovingly and tried to get Grandma back on track.

"Did you know that Mr Falconer had married Rosalie Jordan?" I asked.

"Yes, of course," she replied. "News always gets round. I didn't give it much thought, though when Mary told me they'd had a daughter I remember hoping she wouldn't grow up like Rosalie."

"It was Rosalie's grandson who grew up like her," said Shirley sadly.

I know I'd been slow, but it was only now, suddenly, that the full implication of Grandma's love affair hit me.

"Shirley," I gasped, "does this mean that Zak –"

"Yes," said Shirley, adding quite forcefully, "and before you say it – *don't*."

So I didn't. But I do still wonder whether Zak ever found out how closely he was related to cool, stylish Miss Fairlie – not to mention what his "naive" grandfather actually got up to after the Saturday dance.

Grandma wasn't interested in Zak. Now that she'd got going, her story kept pouring out.

"Last August I saw the announcement of Rosalie's death in the *Herald*. As if I hadn't had enough sadness to bear, that night I felt as if a dam had burst in my mind. Memories of events fifty years ago came flooding back and I couldn't stop them. I kept visualising myself at Goldie's Academy; I heard Hugh singing and saw wee Alice jumping around and cheeking Rosalie Jordan. Lying in my bed at night, I could hear children shouting in the park and trains thundering under Corngate Bridge. They should have been happy memories, but they were all tainted by what happened at the end. I've sat all winter in that horrible, poky little flat, blaming Hugh Falconer, grieving because my girl never knew her real father, crying over the waste of my education and the lie I've lived for fear those I loved would think ill of me. The only peaceful times I've had were when I went to Mary's in December and to stay with Alice last month."

"We had peace then too, didn't we, Shirley?" I said.

Grandma gave us a contrite look.

"I'm so ashamed," she said. "I knew that last day you came to lunch that something was badly wrong, and I meant to visit you, really I did. But even though my mother died forty years ago and Goldie's Academy is long gone, I've never been able to face coming back here. So I left you to be haunted by my thoughts, and preyed on by an evil spirit who saw you and remembered Alice and me. Oh, Shirley –" she covered her face with her hands "– if I had known that you were working for Hugh Falconer –"

"I hate him," I screamed suddenly. "I don't care if he is my grandfather. He's been a pig to Shirley and he wouldn't let her apply for his job, even though everyone says she's the best teacher in the school."

The tension was broken as Shirley burst out laughing.

"Mousie," she teased, "you can write me a reference tomorrow." Then she glanced at Grandma and said, "Don't worry. That's another story."

Grandma disagreed.

"I imagine it's the same story," she said soberly. "When you walked in, he must have seen a ghost too. Oh, Shirley girl," she added passionately, "if only you'd gone to teach somewhere else! I'd have come anywhere in the wide world with you, except Millkennet."

It was strange. Shirley and I hadn't had time to discuss the future, but at that moment each of us knew what was in the other's mind. I let Shirley ask the question.

"Would you come anywhere in the wide world with us now?"

It was obvious, when we'd heard Grandma's answer,

that Shirley wasn't going to be able to sleep. While Grandma made her comfortable, I went to make tea for them and a chicken sandwich for myself, because I was starving. We sat together late into the night, eagerly planning what we were going to do.

27

The Last Haunting

I was sorry, on the last day of term, that Shirley wasn't at school to see me getting my Geography prize. In a way, though, her absence made it easier for me to do something that was important to me. I thought Shirley would disapprove, although later she assured me that how I managed things was entirely my own affair.

The days following Shirley's violent encounter with the ghost hadn't been easy. Apart from slinging tea and toast onto a tray and filling hot-water bottles, I had no experience of looking after an invalid. It soon became clear to me that I had no talent for it. Shirley was restless and irritable, her mood swinging wildly between stoicism and peevishness, hope and despair. I don't know which was harder to handle, her tearful self-pity or her abject remorse afterwards. When I was at freaking-out point, however, Grandma was unsympathetic.

"When you and I couldn't cope," she pointed out, "Shirley looked after us. Now she's in pain and it's our turn to care for her. If we're kind and reassuring, all of this will pass."

Grandma had calmed down a lot since she got her life-story off her chest. I'd never known her so mellow, with only an occasional baring of the fangs to remind us that she was still Boss Woman.

On Monday afternoon, the kids from school started ringing the doorbell. Soon there was a little grey path across the pale gold carpet from the sitting-room door to the sofa where Shirley lay with a blanket tucked round her knees. As usual, she raised her performance for them:

"Oh, I'm so pleased to see you. Come and tell me all the news. Is it true that Mr Falconer's taking my choir to the festival? How is Mr Gibbons getting on with *Twelfth Night*?"

The apartment was full of flowers and get-well cards, and there was a big brown teddy bear wearing granny specs and a blue and white striped scarf. His name was "Millkenneth", and he would live with Shirley for the rest of her life. But when the kids had gone home, she cried and said she didn't know how to tell them what was going to happen.

"Then let someone else tell them," snapped Grandma in a fang-baring moment. "It sounds as if you've had to do everything else."

On Wednesday Granny Clark came to visit Shirley. When she went away, she left a large envelope on the hall table. On it she'd written, "I thought you might like to see yourself in 1952," a joke which misfired, but at least gave us a hint of what the envelope contained. Shirley looked at copies of the photographs of her grandparents with fascination tinged with fear. Wordlessly she handed them to Grandma, who tore them to shreds and threw them away.

"No more looking back," she said.

Shirley and I agreed – and so, it seemed, did Sooty. His duty to Shirley done, the strange animal took no further interest in her, or in me. He had taken up residence with the Huntlys, and passed me snootily on the stair as if we had never met. Considering what the future held, I didn't try to lure him back. Before I could turn away from the past, however, I had a final ghost to confront.

On Friday afternoon, Mr Croy held an assembly so that prizes could be handed out and presentations made to teachers who were leaving Millkennet High for the last time. Because Mr Falconer had been in the school for as long as the war memorial window, Mr Croy had invited him to hand out the sports awards and prizes for the term.

"I've also asked Mr Falconer to choose the prize books," said Mr Croy jovially, "so I hope you prize-winners will approve of his choice."

"*The Beano Annual 1942*," sniggered Rab, who was behind me in the queue.

As I stood waiting my turn, I amused myself wondering what would happen if I said, "Thanks, Granddad," then shoved the principal teacher of English off the platform. By the time I climbed the steps, however, the humour of the situation had faded. When Mr Croy announced, "Second-year Geography project –

Alice Fairlie," I walked up to Mr Falconer and looked him right in the eye. That was when I was sure that he knew me – and that he knew that I knew him.

He said, "Well done," and shook hands with me.

I said, "Thank you, Mr Falconer," and went off to a reasonable round of applause. Only when I got back to my seat and looked down at the book he'd chosen, I couldn't stop laughing. It was *Lorna Doone*.

After we'd filed out of the hall, I went to the cloakroom, emptied my locker and said goodbye to Gillian and Louise. I stood at the front door for a while, watching my schoolmates drift away from me in the thin spring rain. When they were gone, I went back into the hall to wait for my grandfather.

The place was hot and pungent with recently released bodies. I sat on a chair, looking at the ancient dux boards high on the wall. There were two from Goldie's Academy and four from the old Millkennet High School, where children had been quietly educated without paying for three hundred years. It seemed strange that I'd been walking through the hall for two terms, never dreaming that my grandmother's name was inscribed there. The boards were dusty and faded, irrelevant to education in the twenty-first century, but I was still fiercely proud to see *Jean Francis 1952*.

The teachers were in the staff-room next door, drinking tea. I could hear their blah-blah and the clink of teaspoons through the open door. At four o'clock they too began to drift off homewards and I moved into the vestibule. Carrying his raincoat over his arm, Mr

Falconer came out of the staff-room with Mr Croy. They shook hands and, as Mr Croy went off along the corridor, I stepped forward.

"Ah," said Mr Falconer softly. "I thought I might see you again today." He didn't try to avoid me. Sitting down on a bench outside the school office, he gestured to me to sit beside him. "What can I do for you?" he asked resignedly.

"Two things," I said, dumping my book bag and unzipping my fleece. "I want to hear you say you know who I am. And I want to know why you've been so cruel to Shirley."

He didn't like the word "cruel" any more than Grandma had liked "deceived". He rubbed his right foot against his left shin and blinked his faded denim eyes.

"Oh yes, Shirley," he said. "How is she?"

No longer "Miss Fairlie", I observed sourly.

"Still not well," I replied, "but she'll get better. Grandma's looking after her. You haven't answered my question."

I must admit that he wasn't shifty. All the time we were talking, he looked me in the eye.

"I know who you are, Alice," he said. "But how do you know about me? Shirley didn't know."

I hadn't expected this and I had to think quickly.

"I found photographs in the History room," I said, "of you with Grandma and Rosalie Jordan. Mrs Clark told me she was your wife. When Grandma came to nurse Shirley, she told us – about you and her. She thought it was time we knew." Mr Falconer seemed satisfied but didn't say anything, so I pressed on accusingly. "You must have known who Shirley was. Why were you unkind? You made her so unhappy."

This arrow found its mark. He flinched visibly.

"Of course I knew who she was," he said quietly. "When she walked in to be interviewed, I couldn't believe my eyes. She was Jean reborn – the same beauty and intelligence, the same ardour and quiet confidence. I tried to block her appointment but I was outvoted, and no wonder. The rest of the committee were enchanted by her. She had decided to be a teacher and she was going to be the best."

"But you stopped her," I cried angrily.

Mr Falconer tutted impatiently.

"I couldn't stop her," he said. "You can't extinguish sunlight. The children were dazzled by her, and whatever I asked of her she did brilliantly. These last terrible months she couldn't have supported me more generously if she'd known what she was to me. She was a grandchild any man would have been proud of."

He didn't mention Zak, but the comparison hung painfully between us.

"Then why did you treat her so badly?" I asked, less strident but determined to have an answer. "You wouldn't let her apply for your job. You wouldn't even give her a reference."

Mr Falconer fumbled inside his jacket and produced a long envelope.

"I wouldn't give her a reference for my job, because I wanted her out of Millkennet," he said tightly. "This is her reference for any other job in the world. I was going to post it, but you can give it to her, if you like."

"Thanks," I nodded, taking the envelope and dropping it into my book bag. It was a small thing, yet I knew how much it would mean to Shirley. "But I still don't understand. Was it so terrible, having her there? Nothing that happened was her fault."

For a moment, I thought my grandfather was going to cry, but he controlled himself.

"It was deeply painful," he replied, "to be reminded daily of what might have been. When your mother died . . . my daughter . . ." His eyes pleaded for sympathy but, not finding it, he changed tack. "My reason for wanting Shirley to leave wasn't entirely selfish. I was married for nearly forty years to a vindictive, obsessively jealous woman who made sure that the memory of Jean Francis poisoned my life as well as her own. I gave her all any normal person could have wanted, but she was like a snake eating her own deadly tail. I lived in terror of her learning that Jean's granddaughter was teaching in my department. I had plenty of evidence that Rosalie could be violent. I was afraid for Shirley's safety if she ever found out."

I saw him shivering in the grey draught from the door and, remembering Shirley lying on the hall floor, I shivered too.

"Why did you marry Rosalie?" I asked.

I suppose it was an impudent question, but he gave me a truthful, if bitter answer.

"Because I'm a weak man," he confessed. "All my life, I've taken what seemed the easy way at the time. I behaved like a skunk to the most wonderful girl I ever knew because my father threatened to stop funding me and I was afraid of being poor. I married Rosalie for much the same reason; she wanted it, her parents wanted it and my parents were determined it would happen. Anyway, once I'd lost Jean, I really didn't care who I married." His tired eyes looked at me desolately. "When Rosalie died in August," he went on, "I thought I could begin to make up to Shirley for the hurt I knew she felt. But – do you believe in ghosts, Alice?"

"Yes," I said.

"Then perhaps you can imagine what it's like to be haunted. When I got back from her funeral, Rosalie was waiting for me. Every day I saw her, glaring through the kitchen window, standing in doorways, watching my every move. Until last week, the only time I was free of her was in December, when the cat came."

"What cat?" I whispered, swallowing over a lump in my throat.

My grandfather wiped his forehead with a blue-veined hand.

"It was a black cat, a stray," he said. "I fed him for about a month, then he disappeared. Rosalie was terrified of cats, ever since she was attacked by one when she was a girl. I wanted to get one of my own, but my grandson said he would kill it. He didn't like cats either."

My heart was pounding and my head in a spin, but I wasn't entirely speechless. I even managed to keep my voice steady. "You said, until last week," I reminded him.

"Yes." He looked puzzled. "Since last Thursday I haven't seen Rosalie once. I wish I could believe she's gone for good."

Thursday – the day the black cat had avenged us all. I might have been reassuring, but I'd have had to reveal far too much. We sat for a while in silence, staring out into the bald March afternoon. Eventually my grandfather glanced at his watch.

"I have to catch a bus at ten past five," he said, "and you must go home." He got up and put on his coat, while I zipped up my fleece and lifted my bag. We walked together through drizzle to the gate. I'd been feeling quite sorry for him, but then he said something so crass, my heart hardened again. "Do you suppose – while your grandma is in Millkennet, um – she might like me to call on her one day? Just to have a cup of tea, you know, for old times' sake?"

I looked at him in despair. Did he seriously think that the ruin of Grandma's youthful dreams could be patched up in old age over a cup of tea? She was still so afraid of encountering her past, she had scarcely stepped outside Goldie Court since she arrived. It wasn't even worthwhile trying to explain. Whatever remorse Hugh Falconer had felt long ago for his treatment of Jean Francis, now there was nothing but curiosity in his washed-out eyes.

"There'll be no time for that," I told him crisply. "The doctor says Shirley won't be well enough to go back to school next term, so as soon as she can travel we're going to stay with Grandma's friend at Dunoon. Shirley's going to teach me till the summer holidays, then in the autumn we're all going to live in Canada. Shirley's going to University to finish her PhD, though she'll go back to teaching afterwards because it's all she wants to do. I'll go

to school in Ontario, and Grandma will be there for us –
and of course we'll be there for her when she needs us,
later on. Grandma says we can all still have a good life if
we hold hands and walk bravely into the future. She
won't let us live in the past any more."

"Oh, Mousie, I don't think that was very kind," said
Shirley reproachfully, when I repeated this conversation
to her later in the evening. "Did you have to rub it in
quite so hard?"

She had wept when she read the warm, appreciative
things her grandfather had written about her and, ever a
reconciler, was already well on the way to forgiving him.
At the time, I thought he deserved it, but now I'm not so
sure. I see him often in my mind's eye, a lonely old man
with only the past to look forward to, walking away down
Corngate to the bus stop.

THE END